SKY LAKE

A JEFF TAYLOR MYSTERY

Also by Scott Lipanovich

The Lost Coast

The Golden Ceiling

SKY LAKE

A JEFF TAYLOR MYSTERY

Scott Lipanovich

Encircle Publications
Farmington, Maine, U.S.A.

Editor: Cynthia Brackett-Vincent
Cover design by Christopher Wait and Deirdre Wait
Cover photograph © Getty Images

Published by:

Encircle Publications
PO Box 187
Farmington, ME 04938

info@encirclepub.com
http://encirclepub.com

To the memory of Clint Sherman:
teacher; coach; referee; solid tennis player; friend

PART ONE

One

I stepped atop the stone summit of Mount Tallac and gazed down at mile after mile of Lake Tahoe's dreamy, cobalt-blue water. The largest alpine lake in North America, it stretches twenty-two miles north-south, a dozen miles east-west. The California-Nevada border runs approximately down its middle. Surrounded by evergreen forests at six thousand feet above sea level, Tahoe's waters are icy year-round.

Wind flurries pushed me from behind. Ahead, water and sky seemed to converge in a heavenly middle distance. Struck by my insignificance, I thought of how astronauts refer to being overwhelmed by beauty when looking out at planet Earth. Another gust struck. I adjusted my footing so as not to risk tumbling down the rocky chest of the mountain. I experienced what people sometimes do when standing on rooftops or bridges: a momentary desire to jump.

I surveyed the view, seeking to memorize it. Wind blew my baseball cap off. It fluttered in space like a bird. I took this as a sign and did not watch its downward flight. I turned around and, ducking into the chilly wind, began descending the mountain. At the tree line, snow remained in shadowy pockets sunlight never reached. As I dropped in elevation, the trees became thicker, closer together. The trail reached the shore of diminutive Feather Lake. Its grasses were tawny. Trout rose to the surface, leaving bubbles that looked like silvery jewels.

A man emerged from the forest. Head down, he watched his phone. He wore a blue Los Angeles Dodgers baseball cap. He didn't take in my presence until I moved off the path to let him pass.

He looked up. "How many bars you get?"

"I didn't bring my phone."

He looked to the small screen. "I can't get decent reception. It's frustrating as hell."

The man continued walking with his head down. Reflected on the lake's surface were neighboring green treetops; the silvery bubbles speckled them. The man walked past the water, headed uphill. Had he even seen Feather Lake?

An hour later, the trail ended at asphalt. Cathedral Road led to the large cabin my wife, Karen, and I rented at Fallen Leaf Lake, west of the highway that paralleled Lake Tahoe. No cars went by. The wind pushed clumps of brown pine needles along the road, end over end, like small tumbleweeds.

Once indoors, I lit a fire of cedar kindling topped with Douglas fir, heated a lunch of steaming macaroni and cheese, and turned on my laptop. We'd moved in the first week of September, renting what Karen and I called The Lodge, with Karen to begin working as a supervising nurse at Barton Memorial Hospital on October first. I was slated to take the California medical board certification tests beginning on the eighth of October. With Karen visiting family back East, I studied, yes, but I also read local history and followed the local news. Warmed from food followed by ginger tea, I brought up the day's edition of the *Tahoe Daily Tribune*.

The front page headline:

FAMED SKIER FOUND DEAD

Brett Boyd, renowned water skier who resided in the West Tahoe area, was found dead late Wednesday afternoon in his chalet-style cabin at the exclusive enclave Sky Lake Estates. South Lake Tahoe Police Sergeant Jim Stevens discovered Boyd's body. Stevens responded to a call from Boyd's estranged wife, the model Elise Jansen. Jansen had contacted the police after Boyd did not return phone calls or respond to text messages for forty-eight hours.

Though they were separated, Jansen told the police she and Boyd were in almost daily contact.

Boyd was known to suffer from depression, sometimes accompanied by episodes of heavy drinking. Court records show two convictions for driving with a blood alcohol concentration above the legal limit.

Elise Jansen declined a request from the Daily Tribune for an interview.

Straight out of high school, Boyd was a consistent winner in slalom on the professional water skiing circuit. He set the world record three times. Four years ago, a torn hamstring sidelined him for six months. He returned to competition but never regained his previous level of success.

Boyd retired from water skiing and moved full-time to the Sky Lake Estates cabin he and Jansen had purchased during his glory days.

Wintering in the Tahoe Basin rather than water skiing in warmer climes, Boyd took up snow skiing. In

April, he surprised contest organizers by accepting an invitation to the first Cal Ski/Ski competition, where promoters invited five professional snow skiers and five professional water skiers, seven men and three women, to compete in both sports. Broadcast on cable television, the organizers declared winner Bob La Porte the Golden State's Greatest Skier.

Boyd placed third in the competition. He was thirty-two years old. Sergeant Stevens is heading up the investigation into his passing.

Without Karen's good judgment to steady me, I was a mess. Brett, my age, dead? It didn't seem possible. I'd never known anyone more alive. I grabbed a hooded sweatshirt from the back of a chair, went out to my brown Subaru Outback, drove to the highway, and headed north. Slits of light flashed like knives between tall pine and cedar trees. The flashing lights made me lightheaded. The morning's clear sky had turned a gloomy purple. It was like driving into a bruise.

Brett Boyd was dead.

A league rival for three seasons, a teammate on NorCal elite high school basketball teams in spring postseasons, Brett was the best player on Team Far North. We'd pushed each other on the court, drove over twisty country highways on Sundays to play intense games of one-on-one. In a kind of pilgrimage, I took a different country highway to see where Brett had spent his final days.

The newspaper was correct. Sky Lake Estates was exclusive. Down by Lake Tahoe the homes were huge and sold for several millions. The cabins up at Sky Lake, however, were true family vacation homes rarely offered for sale. The road in was gated but the area wasn't fenced. I parked, walked along the highway then cut through a field of prickly waist-high brush toward the baby blue, egg-shaped lake. I pulled on my sweatshirt hood to keep out the chilly wind.

The brush ended at powdery dirt that slanted downward, then became level at a sand volleyball court. Its net and metal poles had been removed and wouldn't be in use again until next summer. Beyond the court were wood houses and a boxy structure with a second story that reminded me of an old fire station built to house one truck. Ahead was the water, stippled with whitecaps raised by an ever-increasing gale. The wind generated a whistling song that swept between tall pines set back from the far side of the lake. Along the near shore a trail led to Sky Falls, water plunging two hundred feet over granite. I'd hiked there a few times with friends while a student at Sacramento State. The place held fond memories—until that afternoon.

Yellow police tape enveloped a cedar chalet with a lofty, steeped roof. Next to it, a detached garage, also cedar, also taped. Those were surely Brett's. I'd had no idea he lived in the Tahoe area. I would have looked him up. Now I'd never see him again.

Remembering how Brett and I called each other *brother* during our teen years, I headed for the taped cabin. A battery-powered cart came from behind the small fire-station-like building and rolled toward me. The driver wore an oversized yellow windbreaker that rippled against the gale. Broad, wrap-around sunglasses blocked view of his eyes and prevented a clear view of his face. His skin shined. Thirty-five years old at most, he conveyed an aggressive bearing while steering the cart.

He yelled into the wind. "You there! Stop!"

I stopped.

He pulled up with the nose of the cart aimed at me. "What are you doing here?"

"Taking a walk along the lake."

He looked at my right hand, which is missing its two smallest fingers, the result of an accident ten years before. The middle finger is a stump too short to flip someone the bird. Out of habit, I slipped the half hand into a pocket. The man's eyes followed it.

He said, "You're trespassing on private property."

The word SECURITY, in chunky black letters, ran down bright yellow nylon from below his shoulder to his wrist. The large windbreaker flapped loudly, like a ship's flag on the open sea. The wind lifted his dark hair like a sail. He wore what appeared to be doe-skin gloves.

I said, "I used to hike here when I was in college. There's a public easement for walking along the lake."

The far larger portion of Sky Lake Estates, down at Lake Tahoe, where tech moguls built mansions, had teams of private security. Curious to see the estates, I'd once started down a road that way and was sent back by men who did not smile when telling me to turn around. That didn't fit the casual atmosphere I'd experienced at Sky Lake, where vacationers waved from porches, relaxed, everyone friendly.

The guy in the yellow windbreaker pointed to the lake. "See the trail marker over there? You're on private property."

The man stood from the driver's seat. Wind billowed the yellow windbreaker. A holstered pistol showed at the man's right hip. "Get going. I mean it."

My pulse quickened. I said, "Have a nice day," and walked to the lakeside path, fighting an urge to look behind me.

What was that about? I'd been looking at what I assumed was Brett's chalet but hadn't gotten close to the yellow caution tape. I figured the man with a pistol on his hip watched my route. The lake narrowed. The wind song grew even louder. Near the end of summer, the water of Sky Falls pattered quietly down boulders that showed stains from eons of melted snow slapping them. My mind circled back to wondering what caused the death of my boyhood friend.

I turned around, retraced my steps. As I approached the cabins, the cart popped around from behind one of them. It rolled up to the chalet I figured was Brett's and halted, with the man positioned between me and the building. He leaned forward onto the steering wheel.

"You've had your walk. Now move along."

"Have a nice day."

"Just move along."

Back at The Lodge, I called Karen. I didn't expect her to understand how upset I was. She grew up among people who jumped horses, took ballet and music lessons, and traveled the globe. It wouldn't be fair to expect her to understand that this poor boondocks kid had exactly one thing of importance in all of his youth: competitive sports. The guys I played with—and against—were my tribe. Among all of them, the most meaningful connection had been with Brett Boyd.

Karen listened to me recount reading about Brett, driving to Sky Lake to check it out, and what happened there.

She said, "That's awful. I know how much you admired him. And thought about him, even after you lost contact."

"My fault. Totally my fault."

"Don't focus on that. He knew about your hand, right?"

"Yeah."

"So he had some understanding of why you broke off contact. Not only with him but with everyone."

My cheeks burned. Brett Boyd was dead.

"That security guard pisses me off."

"Forget him. He's just one of those people who enjoy pushing others around."

The conversation moved to the trek up Mt. Tallac. The incredible views of Lake Tahoe, the stone path above the tree line. Then Karen described the historic inn her family rented for its reunion. She poked fun at the claims in its brochure. We said our goodbyes.

Chomping on French bread and cheddar cheese, my mind replaying what happened at Sky Lake, the food didn't go down easily. Though weary from the Mt. Tallac hike, five miles each way, followed by the walk at Sky Lake, I wasn't able to relax. I could understand having someone keep an eye on Brett's place, but the unnecessary hostility didn't seem the work of a professional security guard. Why hadn't the man identified himself? I lit another fire and walked in circles in a woodsy living room larger than the converted little barn I'd grown up in. I turned on my laptop with not a moment's thought of reviewing for the state boards.

There was no website for Sky Lake Estates, which was a haven for people who valued retreats undisturbed by the outside world. Throwing different words into searches, I came upon a LinkedIn profile of a Frank Baumer. Retired from a career with the Alameda County planning department—in the San Francisco Bay Area— his profile listed him as chair of the Sky Lake Estates Owners Association. After that, it didn't take much sleuthing to find his phone number.

I sat with a pen and notebook and tapped the number.

A friendly male voice: "Frank Baumer."

I introduced myself, told him where I was living, and managed to add I was about to take the state exams for my medical license.

"Congratulations. What's the reason for your call?"

I began recounting what happened at Sky Lake. Baumer politely interrupted.

"You sure you're talking about Sky itself, not down at Tahoe? Those tech folks hire guys who can be aggressive."

I assured him I was talking about egg-shaped Sky Lake.

Baumer chuckled politely. "That's impossible. A fellow named Randy Zim spends the summer there. He takes care of a little of everything. Flat tires, engines that won't start, splitting firewood. And plumbing. Those old places are one plumbing challenge after another. Zim's retired from the trade, in his sixties. He'd never act like the man you describe."

"I'd put the guy at early to middle thirties."

Again, a genial chuckle. "We've done this for years. Zim arrives the second Saturday in May. He gets the grounds ready for Memorial Weekend, our annual opening. He stays on the week after Labor Day, closing up everything. He locks the main gate. Calls me and says, 'See you in May.'"

"Then this wasn't Randy Zim."

Baumer said, "If he forgot something and came back to button it up, it's possible he could be there today. Who else would be riding around in the cart?"

"I don't know. But this guy had a gun on his right hip, and he was nowhere close to his sixties."

Baumer cleared his throat. "I don't know anything about you or what you say. I'm a hundred and fifty miles away, so I'm going to give you a number to call. A sergeant with South Lake Tahoe police. You have a pen?"

"Of course."

Baumer recited a phone number for Sergeant Stevens, the man the newspaper cited as heading the police department's inquiry into Brett's death. Baumer added, "Jim grew up in South Tahoe.

He knows everybody. I'll call him at home. I'll let him know you'll contact him on his cell first thing in the morning. Agreed?"

"Will do. One more thing. What have you heard about Brett Boyd?"

"I hope it's not another drunk driving. You need to be able to drive out once in a while if you're going to winter up there."

I said, "Brett was found dead yesterday afternoon at his place."

Baumer barked into the phone. "Don't you screw with me. Brett's a friend. He's got problems. He drinks too much. Probably other stuff. But if this is some kind of sick joke, I have your number. I'll report it as harassment."

"Mr. Baumer, this is not something I'd joke about. I knew Brett well when we were kids. We were basketball buddies from different small towns way up north."

Baumer's voice lowered. "Wait a second." He sounded bewildered. He breathed into the phone. "Did you say your name is Jeff Taylor?"

"Yes."

"I'll be damned. There's a photograph in Brett's living room. He had it blown up huge. It's a high school basketball team. Everyone's name is printed below them. When I pop in to see him, and he's liquored up, Brett spends more time talking about high school basketball than being a world-champion water skier. He says that's when sports were still fun. I let him go on because, you know, he's alone so much. I've probably heard the name Jeff Taylor ten times. You're saying that's you?"

"Want me to name the other guys in the picture?"

Baumer said, "If you'll excuse me, I've got to call Jim Stevens."

Two

Housed in a low building with walls of brown rock, the South Lake Tahoe Police Department was a block away from the city's bustling commercial district. To the east, on the Nevada side of the border, lofty casinos lined Highway 50. I'd left the soft azure world of Lake Tahoe serenity.

Inside the police department, all was cool efficiency. I produced my driver's license, which was scanned, then set wallet, belt, keys, and phone in a plastic tray that passed through a metal detector. A deputy led me to an office Stevens shared with one woman and one man. All three wore crisp dark blue police uniforms and faced computer screens.

The guy who led me announced, "A man here to see you, Sergeant. Says he talked to you earlier. Says he's expected."

Stevens stood. He had a gray buzz cut and looked to be chasing forty years old. He opened the top drawer of a metal desk and extracted a key ring that barely fit in his right front pocket. He shut the drawer, walked around the desk, and offered a hand. "Jim Stevens."

"Jeff Taylor."

We shook. He gave my hand a double take.

Six feet tall, wearing rectangular, black-framed glasses, Stevens was no-nonsense. He scooped a patrolman's cap off the metal desk and motioned for me to go first. He carried the hat as we walked. "Frank Baumer sounded worried last night. Tell me about it on the way." At the doorway, Stevens looked back to his colleagues. "We'll be at Sky. Shouldn't take more than an hour."

Before he flipped on his cap, I caught sight of a gray cowlick that wound a tight spiral where other guys might have a left-side part. His eyes were hazel and questioning. Thin for a police officer, Stevens didn't speak as we walked to a white patrol car. Once seatbelts clicked, he backed around half a circle. Stevens pulled onto a short road that took us to the highway.

He said, "About yesterday."

His eyes did not stray from the road. The rest of him didn't move, either; he looked like a statue behind the wheel. I recounted going to Sky Lake. Stevens didn't speak again until I said the guy in a yellow windbreaker had a gun on his hip.

"You're sure it was a gun? Not something clipped to, like, a tool belt?"

"It wasn't a garden trowel. I can tell you that. It wasn't a big pistol like a forty-five, or a little twenty-two popper."

Stevens said, "Do you know a lot about firearms?"

"Enough to know the difference between a pistol and a garden trowel."

"Fair enough. Continue."

I told him about the rest of my time at Sky Lake. Stevens didn't say another word until after he pulled left across the highway onto an unmarked dirt road and stopped at an iron pole that blocked our way. Drooping from the end of the pole was a short rope with a knotted loop at its end.

Stevens labored to free the thick key ring from his pocket. It contained perhaps twenty keys. They clanked as he handed them to me. His thumb and forefinger pinched a large one.

"It opens forward. Put the rope around that red post."

I took the keys and got out of the car. The unsophisticated setup fit the informal atmosphere of the small summer community at Sky Lake. Stevens poked his head out of the driver's window.

"Leave it open. Nobody'll be coming."

I climbed back in the car. We bounced on a road that rose up, then leveled, heading past the first summer houses. Looking across the lake, I saw pattering Sky Falls, and white granite running straight up and over the mountain. At my pointing, Stevens stopped in front of the two-story building the cart first came from behind. We got out. Doors shut. The sounds echoed, followed by silence. I wondered how living alone out there all winter—much of it when the dirt road would not be passable—how had that affected Brett? I remembered him as the life of any party, not a recluse like Frank Baumer described.

I returned the keys to Stevens. He shook the ring, found the one he wanted. He unlocked the door to the building and swung it inward. Stevens stepped inside onto the cement. He popped open an electrical panel, engaged the breakers, then flipped on the lights.

Downstairs was a garage/workshop. At its back end, a wide door had a broad handle that opened outwards. Tools were spaced evenly along the side walls. A window, shuttered outside by hooked-on boards, faced the lake and cabins. Adjacent to the window was a plywood counter. The concrete floor was clean enough to play shuffleboard on. Between us and the back door sat a battery-powered cart.

I stepped to the cart. "This is it."

Stevens went to the cart, looked at the driver's chair, then looked at the back bench seat. He examined the key that engaged the battery. He shrugged.

I took a small flashlight from the front pocket of my jeans and shined it into every shadow. Down around the pedal that powered the cart were a few brown leaves and dust.

I handed the flashlight to Stevens, pointed to the leaves. "What do you think? Every other inch in here is spotless."

"That's not exactly what anybody would call a mess."

"Just noting."

Stevens said, "Frank described you as a young doctor."

"Going to be. I used to be a private snoop."

A slight nod. "Let's go upstairs."

The room was smaller than expected, with a slanted roof making the side walls not more than six feet high. Its windows had wood shutters that closed from the outside and latched to the window frames. In the room were a bed and dresser, a small square table with an unplugged reading lamp, and an unplugged space heater stored in a corner. A homemade counter housed a fancy-looking hotplate and a microwave oven. Under the counter was a little refrigerator. On the dresser was a row of paperback books between copper bookends. Everything was neat as an army barracks awaiting inspection. The bathroom sink and shower stall shined.

"This is where Zim lives during summer?"

This garnered a major nod of perhaps two inches.

Stevens said, "Let's go to Brett's. Frank asked me to check out a picture you claim to be in. Of a basketball team. I've seen it but never really looked."

"That's how I knew Brett."

Stevens probably wondered how I'd played basketball with the freakish hand. He gestured for me to head down the stairs. Stevens turned off the lights, disengaged the breakers, and click-closed the metal panel. We went outside. Stevens checked to confirm the door locked. He rummaged through the horde of keys as we walked toward shiny yellow police tape. Our footsteps crunched sand on the volleyball court. A squirrel glanced our way, hesitated, and raced off. We went to the back of Brett's chalet. Stevens casually tore away yellow police tape crossing the back door. He slid a key into the lock.

I said, "That's a boatload of keys."

"Before Brett started staying winters, no one was here from mid-September to mid-May. Several of the owners wanted somebody to have access to their cabins in case of an emergency."

Stevens turned on the lights. It felt peculiar, especially under the circumstances, to step into Brett's home. Piled everywhere were magazines, maps, and guidebooks. A mound of dirty dishes rose precariously above the edge of the kitchen sink. A woodstove was encircled by wood splinters and bark chips. Photographs hung at odd angles on cedar walls.

The house smelled of lengthy neglect.

Stevens said, "Keep your hands in your pockets. That way, you won't touch anything. The print team was here, but they may need to come back. We haven't gotten results. The toxicology report won't be completed till at least Monday. As of now, we don't have a cause of death. The place sits in limbo till we do. Over there," he said, "is the picture Baumer wants me to look at."

My eyes caught the enlarged photograph. I'd once had a smaller copy. Lined up on a basketball court, we were tall kids from small towns from the far north of California who beat elite clubs up and down the state. Names magical to me were written in black ink below each player: David Brown; Bob Koury; Brett in number eleven and me next to him wearing number fifteen; Gary Patterson; Tom Vercelli; Marc Reisfelt; Steve Wilhite; Ralph Nilssen; Mike Madrid. Everyone but Brett went on to play in college. The photograph drew me, tunnel-like, into years of triumph before my hand was wrecked working the night shift the summer after graduating from college during the Sacramento Valley tomato harvest.

Tilting his head, Stevens stepped to the picture. "That's definitely you. You had a little more hair, but it's you."

I said, "Those are some of the best people I've ever known. Over time, I lost touch with them."

Stevens surprised me. He put a hand on my shoulder. "One thing I've learned is it doesn't get easier."

"Losing people?"

"That does get easier. What doesn't is feeling the passage of time." He let go of my shoulder. "You can take a last look. Hands in pockets. I'll be back in a minute."

I wandered inside. I wasn't really looking for anything. Mostly what I saw brought to mind the same word: chaos.

I glanced at the damnable hand. I wished Karen were there. She'd straighten the ship. She always did. Going back through the chalet, my eyes caught something glinting among the clutter on the dining table. It stuck out because, unlike everything else, it looked new. A small white box, about six inches by eight inches, with the lid gone, contained a silver-plated belt buckle resting on white tissue paper. I leaned over to see and reached out, nearly forgetting the order not to touch anything. The belt buckle had a rectangular box etched onto it. Stamped above the box: *Think Outside Of The...* It was simple yet classy. It looked expensive and was unquestionably new.

Stevens came inside and turned off the lights. He held a roll of shiny yellow tape with *Police Line Do Not Cross* printed on it. He locked the back door and wrapped tape around the backside of the cabin.

I said, "You fingerprinted the house and, I assume, Brett's garage. What about the other garage? I swear that's the cart the guy was in.

How about if you check it for fingerprints?"

Stevens scowled. Like a lot of people who live their whole lives in the mountains, his face looked older than the rest of him. The dry air and high-altitude sun tended to make for leathery skin.

He said, "Without evidence, we can't take the time. We can't keep up as it is. You wouldn't believe the number of cars that get stolen down by the casinos. They all have to be printed when they turn up."

"What about the guy who accosted me?"

"Number one, in a similar building down by Tahoe, the Sky Lake Estates Owners Association keeps two carts exactly like the one up here. Number two, the billionaires there, they want to hire the best. They end up getting people like ex-Navy SEALs. These guys are trained to fight lions. Here they get puppies. Teenagers trying to sneak a dinghy on the lake with a six-pack. Guarantee you, this guy was driving around looking for a situation to poke his nose in. A clue is the oversized sunglasses. They all wear 'em. It's a power thing. They can see you, but you can't see them."

"Whoever it was, he got off on intimidating me. Why else let the gun show?"

We reached the white patrol car. In that near silence, the shutting of doors sounded like slams.

Stevens said, "Did he mention Brett by name?"

"No."

That provoked a nod, which I took to mean Stevens thought he'd made a point. He started the engine, then made a U-turn. His eyes stayed on the road. I locked the gate behind us.

Halfway to the police station, Stevens said, "Brett and his ex— they're not legally divorced—talked Sunday night. Then no further communication. Where were you all day Monday and Tuesday?"

"What are you implying?"

"It's a straightforward question. What brought you to Sky Lake?"

I tried to keep my voice calm. "I've been reviewing medical cases ten hours a day for the state exams. I was going stir-crazy. So yesterday morning I hiked Mt. Tallac. When I got back, I wasn't ready to start studying. I poked around on my laptop, saw an article about Brett's death. I came to see where he lived."

We didn't speak the rest of the way to the police department. We got out and shook hands. I drove to Fallen Leaf Lake. I prepped for the state boards. Outside, blue jays squawked. They hopped across the porch railing in search of bread scraps. Their demands would not be denied. By the time I finally got them to shut up, the jays had devoured all the bread in the house, and I was crying.

I hadn't cried since childhood. I hadn't allowed it. This protected me from truths. Brett's death got mixed in with not meeting my father until two months before he died, a father whose very existence was never acknowledged by my mom. A father who turned out to be a fine man, and I hadn't had him in my life until his time was short.

Finally, after a decade, I let loose, wailing over the damage to my right hand. Until then, I hadn't had the courage to feel the depth of losing what had allowed me to overcome a childhood spent off the grid in a converted barn. That hand had paid my way through college. It had given me years of joy on basketball courts all over the West… which brought my careening emotions back to Brett Boyd.

We'd kept in touch while I played at Sacramento State and Brett toured the world competing in water ski tournaments. We saw each other during winter holidays. After my hand got trashed, I cut communications with everyone. I developed a bunker mentality, seeing no one other than who was necessary while working for Sherman Investigations, the place I'd landed when Clint, the owner, took me on after I couldn't face going to medical school with half a hand. I became accustomed to living a shadowy sort of life, not just snooping on people, but becoming well versed in online worlds where almost anything desired could eventually be uncovered.

By then Brett was a celebrity, a young guy flying high. He finally gave up trying to make contact.

It was at about that time I saw an article in *Sports Illustrated* titled "Wild Man Boyd." It described Brett's escapades on the water ski circuit. I'd thought about checking in, to make sure he wasn't out of control. I knew how quickly life can go south. But I'd been too immersed in my personal pity party to simply text my friend and suggest he slow down, and ask if he wanted to talk. I'd screwed up by not reaching out. We may not be our brother's keeper, but at times we sure as hell should try to help.

Three

"No Senora Karen? When she's here, the room gets lights."

"She's visiting family back East. It's her first long vacation in years."

"When the Senora come back, I bring a big meal. On the house."

With Antonio, of Antonio's, every meal was offered gratis. On the way out either Karen or I would drop money behind the high counter at the cash register. We or Antonio never spoke of it. From the fourth of July on, Karen and I had spent every weekend in South Lake Tahoe. Preparing to leave Sacramento, we scouted our future, staying at a motel on the highway walking distance to Antonio's.

Thick around the middle, a bulge oozed over Antonio's white belt. His dark cheeks were chubby. Always impeccably groomed, Antonio spoke with a lyrical accent and operated a wonderful restaurant. We came to know each other in the same way Antonio came to know other regulars. He pulled up a chair after a meal was finished and initiated conversation.

One evening, rather than pull up a chair, Antonio asked Karen and me to accompany him to the kitchen. His mother had tripped on the back stair and twisted an ankle. Antonio made a circle with his hands, indicating its swelling. Karen told Mrs. Ramirez to soak the ankle in ice for fifteen minutes. Wait an hour, then repeat. Wait two hours and repeat again. The next day, at a medical supply store, I found a walking boot that looked to be the right size. We brought it that night. Thereafter, the waiters were not allowed to offer menus. Antonio saw to our meals himself.

The day Antonio asked after Karen, I asked if some of his customers worked security in the area. Antonio asked why I wanted to know. I said I'd been up at Sky Lake, and a security guard wearing a pistol told me to get lost.

Antonio's smile was generous. "Let's go in back and see how my mom is doing. Thank you for helping with her ankle."

Antonio's mom's ankle had been perfectly fine for weeks. I followed him past the counter, through the swinging door where trays of hot food—melted cheeses, black beans, peppers of every kind, their smells rich—were carried out by waiters in all white. On their heads: red pirate hats. At Antonio's, a good performance accompanied the good food.

We went to a small office with a phone, computer and ledgers on a desk that consumed half of the space. I took the one wood chair shoved close to the desk.

Antonio said, "What you need, if I can help, it is done."

I said I was looking for someone, and described what happened at Sky Lake. Antonio picked up a small metal file and smoothed the ends of his fingernails. I described the yellow nylon jacket with the word SECURITY running down its right arm. Antonio ceased the fingernail filing. He raised the file like a conductor's baton, was about to speak, then didn't. He set the file on his desk. He plucked a business card from a stack, leaned over and wrote on the card.

Antonio said, "I cannot help you, but maybe my brother can. His name is Roberto. This is his line of work. Tell him what you told me."

"How do I make contact?"

"I take care of that. He is my brother. Can you go now?"

"Right now?"

"When a gun is involved, you don't worry about scheduling. Go to Blizzard Casino. It's four miles on the other side." This meant across the state line, in Nevada. "Give this to the man at the parking lot."

Antonio handed me his business card. On it he'd written: *Roberto waiting for him. Antonio.*

I left without eating lunch.

Traffic slowed shortly before I crossed into Nevada. The afternoon had turned cool. Sunlight, however, ricocheted off the high windows of iconic Harvey's Hotel and Casino. I passed smaller Dotty's, then MontBleu, several more. Near the end of town I came upon Blizzard, a newer, slicker-looking building than the others, four stories of a cobalt-blue exterior I assumed was meant to represent the waters of Lake Tahoe. Its neighbors were a restaurant offering a Silver Dollar Din-Din for $8.99, a motel that promised honeymooners discount rates, and a monstrous, pea-green store called Take and Save that appeared to be doing brisk business.

At Blizzard Casino I stopped at a kiosk with a black-and-white striped gate, like at a railroad crossing. The man who leaned out of the glassed box wore a bright yellow windbreaker. In black along its right arm: SECURITY. I handed him Antonio's card. The man examined it.

"Welcome, sir. Park anywhere not marked handicapped."

Now I understood Antonio's reaction after I mentioned the yellow windbreaker.

I parked. At the casino's entrance, a man and a woman, in yellow windbreakers, stood watch. Inside, the air was artificially chilled and carried wafts of cigarette smoke. I asked a young woman wearing a Blizzard lanyard where I could find Roberto Ramirez. I handed her Antonio's card. Again it was examined.

"Come this way."

We traversed a room larger than any church I'd been in. Colored lights flashed as bells clanged from every kind of gambling machine. The last stretch had tables for poker, blackjack and craps. The woman knocked at an unmarked door. She let me in and disappeared.

Roberto stood. His smile equaled Antonio's, though at the same time he seemed to take my measure. In a dark suit, white shirt, black tie, no extra girth pooched out at the waist. A diamond earring twinkled in the lobe of his left ear.

"You are Jeff Taylor. Welcome."

I walked under banks of video screens broadcasting spots on two gaming floors. I went to a wide desk. An opened laptop sat in its center. Rather than a keyboard, what looked like a music studio's mixing board ran across the desk's length. We shook hands. Roberto didn't flinch. Antonio must have given him a heads up.

I sat.

Roberto said, "My brother says you have a need."

For the fourth time, to Baumer, Stevens, Antonio and then Roberto Ramirez, I recounted what happened at Sky Lake. This time, not a word of interruption. The longer I sat across from Roberto, the more a resemblance between brothers showed. And the longer I sat there, the stranger it felt to be surrounded by TV screens broadcasting black-and-white images of people chasing money.

Roberto said, "If that man works for us, he will be gone." Roberto tapped laptop keys. "Here." He lifted the laptop, turned it around and handed it to me. "Hit the right arrow for next photo. If any seem like your guy, I'll look into it."

I clicked through mug shots. After about a hundred, the faces blurred from one into the next. Between the wrap-around sunglasses, the gale and the swift aggressiveness of the man in question, I hadn't gotten much of a look at him.

"None of these jump out."

Roberto said, "Keep in mind we have high turnover. Every winter we lay off ten percent of staff. Another five percent just move on. The long and short is, a small army of people who don't work here anymore have Blizzard windbreakers."

We shook. Roberto handed me a business card. "If anything else comes up, call. You helped our mother."

I drove back to South Lake Tahoe, turned right at two-lane Highway 89 and motored up the west side of the lake. I lowered a window and received the rich scents of a forest. Before reaching the road to our rented cabin, black smoke spread above treetops. The road grew twisty. From behind came a howling siren. In the rear-view mirror a red pickup truck raced toward me. Red lights flashed across its top. I skidded onto a dirt turnout and the truck zoomed past.

Heading in the direction of the smoke, I passed the unmarked road I'd taken with Sergeant Stevens. Made a broad left turn and parked. Blackish smoke drifted overhead. The air smelled like a summer campfire, but this was no marshmallow roast. I jogged across the narrow highway, raised my arms and cut through the waist-high brush. Coming over a rise in the land, I saw two fire trucks and eight firefighters in black hard hats hosing down Brett's chalet and detached garage. Nobody moved fast, knocked out windows or chopped into doors. It was mop up. The house's roof sagged. The whole place sagged. The detached garage had burned to the ground. The buildings, close to the water, didn't threaten the forest.

Sergeant Stevens stood next to a police car, resting his back against its hood. Next to him stood a man about fifty wearing a white firefighter captain's hat. Behind him rested the red pickup that had zoomed past me. I looked at the charred chalet and gutted garage, and walked to Stevens. He nodded.

I said hello to him and the fire chief.

Stevens took off his patrolman's cap and ran a hand back through the marine-cut gray hair. "Why do you keep showing up at a crime scene?"

Stevens did not introduce me to the fire chief, who instead of saying hello leaned to his right and watched the crew at work.

I said, "Assuming this is arson, isn't it my first visit to a crime scene?"

"Regarding Brett, initial testing led to a conclusion of accidental overdose, alcohol and fentanyl. But we got a new woman in the lab. Something about the amounts didn't make sense to her. Brett was young, and for all his bad habits in good physical condition. She ran a different set of tests and found potassium cyanide. Combined with alcohol and fentanyl, it wouldn't take much to kill him. No hints of suicide. And now this," Stevens said, pointing to the scorched buildings. "It looks like someone killed Brett. It'll get in the papers. That's the new transparency. Make sure the perp gets everything we do."

"I would've never imagined any of this in Brett's life. The hard partying, yes. Not this."

The fire chief flashed a palm as a goodbye, and headed for the skeletal remains of house and garage.

The fire chief said, "Jim."

Stevens said, "Art."

I wondered if South Lake Tahoe first responders took a course in communicating with as few words as possible.

Stevens turned from watching the mop up. "Where are you coming from?"

"Blizzard Casino." I fished out Roberto's card. "I found out about the yellow windbreaker. Kind of."

"Yeah?"

I explained that everyone involved in security at Blizzard wore a yellow windbreaker. And that with regular turnover in the ranks, over the years a lot of them would be floating about. I told Stevens I'd looked at mug shots of the staff, and no one stood out as the man who accosted me.

Stevens said, "I'm surprised he let you look. You're not law enforcement."

"My wife and I helped his mom with a health situation."

"If you helped my mom with a health situation, I wouldn't let you look at pictures of staff. That's crossing a line."

"You're in law enforcement."

Stevens said, "Don't start thinking you are."

"What can you tell me about the fires?"

"Same as the newspapers will. By how they burned, the chief says they're insiders, meaning they started from within. Fast as it went, an accelerant was spread throughout. We'll have a specialist investigate, but there's pretty much nothing left to see."

"What about footprints?"

Stevens pointed to the firefighters. "Millions of 'em."

"Any perpetrators in mind?"

"I approach every case the same," Stevens said. "Everyone is a suspect except me."

I gave Stevens one of his mini nods, said goodbye and walked across the summer volleyball court. I pushed my way through the high spiky brush to Highway 89.

Waiting for an opening in traffic, to jog to my car, I saw a man standing on the ridge above the other side of the curving highway. He looked through binoculars. The binoculars pointed toward

Sky Lake. The fires were arson. Sergeant Stevens said Brett had been poisoned. In my mind, the spreading black smoke overhead proved Brett was murdered.

I reached my car and headed up the road. The first switchback coincided with a rise in elevation. At the second switchback was a fine though short-lived view of Lake Tahoe. Curling back, the road leveled off. I passed the man using binoculars. Short spiky dark hair covered his head like a carpet. Skinny sideburns grew down to cheekbones. Standing ahead of a clean white pickup, he wore jeans and a blue work shirt. A company's name I didn't catch was painted across the truck's side. Attached behind the cab window, a black steel toolbox.

It wasn't the guy who confronted me at Sky Lake. I drove to the Emerald Bay lookout site. I drove a loop in the parking lot, halted at the exit and looked for an opening in traffic.

A California Highway Patrol car passed. I pulled out and headed for Fallen Leaf Lake.

The white pickup truck was gone. Less than thirty seconds after a police vehicle drove by. The pickup was already replaced by a sedan out of which spilled people wearing colorful vacation clothes. They brandished iPhones and cameras and watched the black smoke rising above Sky Lake.

I descended the switchbacks. At level ground trees flitted by on both sides. The highway entered a straight stretch. I craned my neck out the open window but didn't see the back of the pickup with a black toolbox bolted to its bed.

Traffic stalled at an area called Camp Cunningham: a rustic inn, grocery store, bike rental, beach and pier, and a campground on the other side of the highway. I rocked forward and back, impatient with the brief traffic jam. Six miles later, a white pickup turned left into a residential section of South Lake Tahoe. Trees, no sidewalks, modest houses on modest lots. A cozy neighborhood. I located the pickup truck in front of a brown shingled house, and parked. Curious about the truck's swift departure after the passing of a California Highway Patrol car, I walked toward the front door with no plan in mind.

Whitmer Electric and a state contractor's license number were painted in black across the pickup's side. A concrete front porch had an eight-foot overhang. A lamp hung dead center in the outdoor ceiling. The porch and asphalt driveway appeared recently poured. I knocked on the screen door frame harder than intended because of rushing adrenaline.

A heavy brown door swung inward with a pleasant groan. The man with short spiky hair and long narrow sideburns appeared. Behind him a television emitted shooting sounds. He offered the empty reflexive smile one gives a stranger. In his right hand was a triangle of pizza. I placed him at about forty-five years old.

He said hello while chewing and holding the pizza slice midway between his mouth and belly.

"I saw you turn off the highway. I was wondering." I looked to my feet. "I don't know how to put it."

"Did someone send you?"

At that point, all I knew was Brett was dead, there were drugs in his system and poison, too. "Brett Boyd sent me."

The man swallowed, stepped back, looked me over.

"Brett's an old friend," I said.

"Do you know about what happened?"

"Yes."

He pointed to my half hand. "You're not with the police. Not likely, anyway." His voice was smooth, like a radio announcer's.

"That's right. I'm not."

I watched as closely as I could with him in the semi-darkness of the house. Dramatic music came from the TV. That he'd looked to see what I had in hand put me on alert.

He said, "What do you want?"

"What do you got?"

A smile bloomed, larger than the first one, yet still vacant. "Not here. Brett shouldn't have told you to come here."

I shrugged. "What can I say?"

The man went to the living room, set the pizza slice back in its slot, turned the sound off a big-screen TV sitting on what otherwise would be a dining room table. He returned to the screen door, unlocked it. "How about if you get off the porch and tell me about being friends with Brett?"

I swung the screen door outward, and entered the house. The furniture was all a bright leprechaun green. A redwood burl coffee table held a plate of pizza slices. Next to it was a can of Diet Coke, a TV remote control, and a phone. On the walls were framed posters of Star Wars movies, eight in total. On the surfaces of side tables and a bookshelf were Star Wars figurines. The heavy door shut behind me. The man motioned for me to take a seat. He sat in front of what I assumed was rubbery microwaved pizza. He hadn't had time to heat a pizza in the oven. A scene from a Star Wars movie I didn't recognize played silently on the big television. The cell phone played a cartoon involving what appeared to be zebras.

He said, "Billy Whitmer," lifted a slice and took a hearty bite. He looked to the TV. At one end of the dining table was a vial, like for a prescription. It had a white cap but was not labeled.

I sat. "Jeff Taylor. Brett and I played basketball together. We were best friends our last three years in high school. Then he went on the water ski circuit, and we lost touch over the years."

"Brett told me he liked B-ball more than skiing. He just wasn't good enough to make a living at it."

"He was great. But that's correct. He wasn't NBA material. None of us were."

Whitmer gestured to the pizza.

"No thanks." In my head I heard, *Not here. Brett shouldn't have told you to come here.* I took a shot: "Brett said you were his dealer."

The pizza triangle dropped onto others. Whitmer's face turned a burnished red. "Brett Boyd and I were bros. Two years ago, I installed a new electrical panel at his place—he and his wife's—at Sky Lake. We developed a friendship."

"One where he bought, and you sold? That's what he told me. I asked him where I might find good shit."

The phrase *good shit* seemed to flatter my host. He said, "Have you ever heard the expression, 'A friend with weed is a friend indeed?'"

Whitmer laughed at his quip. He pinched the tip of his nose and looked to the action on the silent TV.

I said, "Have you ever heard the expression 'You're under arrest?'"

Whitmer swallowed Diet Coke. He stood. "Listen, man. I get up early and work hard. Just came home for a late lunch, then I'm back on the job till dark. I'm only talking to you because you say you're an old friend of Brett's."

I stood. I was six inches taller than Whitmer. It didn't daunt him. "You sold dope to Brett. Brett died with dope in his system—and I see you looking down at the fire site half an hour ago. Maybe you were worried the police would find something at Brett's that ties you to dealing. Maybe that makes you an arson suspect."

Whitmer stayed on his feet. His eyes were the same dark brown as his carpet hair and long sideburns. "I don't think you're going to the cops, or you would've already. Besides, I was up at Homewood at seven, on a job. Three witnesses. You've got nothing of value to tell. Why don't we cut the crap and put cards on the table?"

30

"I'll take a slice now."

Whitmer headed for the kitchen. Without looking back, he said, "What was his number in basketball?"

"Eleven."

"What's the most points he scored in a game?"

"Far as I know, fifty-two. Against a team from Orange County."

Passing the table with the big-screen TV on it, Whitmer slipped the dark vial into a jeans pocket. He returned with an empty plate and an unopened Diet Coke.

I set the can on the floor to my left, loaded the plate with two pizza slices, sat across from Whitmer with the plate balanced on my thighs. I confessed that Brett never mentioned him, that I'd moved to Fallen Leaf Lake less than a month before, read about Brett's death, got curious and sentimental. I said I'd previously worked for a private detective agency, and that had influenced me in getting curious regarding Brett's demise. None of this got a reaction. As in zilch.

I put another card on the table: "Are you worried Brett might have died from crap you sold him?"

"Hey, man. I'm super strict about my inventory. Once it's out of my hands, it's out of my control. You know?"

"I know one thing. Brett's dead and you sold him drugs."

Whitmer took a breath, opened his mouth, held back on a retort. Then he said, "Once you got past his brush off, Brett was one of the coolest dudes around. If he wasn't too drunk, he told great stories about water skiing all over the world. We had a lot of laughs. He just got off track in life. It happens to people."

People like you, I thought.

Whitmer glanced at the big TV again.

I described my encounter with the man in the yellow windbreaker. Even when I mentioned the pistol at the man's hip, Whitmer seemed nonplussed. Perhaps in his universe such a thing was not a shock. He looked up, and tugged at the end of the long dark sideburn running down his right cheek.

"Which are your favorites?" Whitmer slowly moved his hand, forefinger pointing at one after another of the Star Wars posters behind me, then back over his head. "I mean favorite movies, not posters."

For someone who said he considered Brett a good buddy, this was a quick change in conversation. Beneath the smooth radio announcer's voice I thought I detected a certain vacancy, like his brain was missing a part. Or his heart.

"I'm not much of a fan. I saw a few at movie nights in college. Didn't see the last several."

"C'mon. This isn't a test."

"You mean a second test. After what was Brett's number and most points in a game."

The hollow smile. Another tug on the long sideburn. "Okay. But this one's just for fun."

"'The Empire Strikes Back,' and the first one."

Whitmer threw his arms open. "Old school! You passed! Let's see what we can do about finding out what happened to Brett."

We exchanged phone numbers. When I left, we did not shake hands.

At the Lodge, I popped open a bottle of beer and sat on the rear deck. Ahead and below, splendid Fallen Leaf Lake. A forested mountain rose on the other side. A gentle breeze carried the sweet smell of pine trees. Everything around me was peaceful. I was not peaceful.

I had no idea what to make of Billy Whitmer.

I called Jim Stevens. His hello came across as not wanting the call.

"Do you know a Bill, or William Whitmer?

"Billy. Electrician. What about him?"

"When I left Sky Lake today, I saw someone on the ridge looking down with binoculars. It's almost impossible to make a U-turn on the highway, so I drove up to turn around at Emerald Bay lookout. I pass the guy with binoculars. He's standing in front of a truck with Whitmer Electric on its side." I lied about seeing the company name at that time to avoid saying I'd followed Whitmer to his house, let alone gone in and spoken with him. "I drive into the Emerald Bay lookout. While waiting to get back on 89, a CHP goes by. When I go by where the guy with the binoculars was, he's gone. Thirty seconds after a police car passed him. I looked up the company name, and found William Whitmer is the owner."

"And this tells me?"

"I thought the police welcomed tips. The man's checking out the fire scene, and he splits as soon as a police car is in the vicinity."

"We appreciate tips. This is an observation."

I thought: To hell with Sergeant Stevens. I wasn't going to give him Whitmer as Brett's dealer. One visit from the police would stop any future information coming from Billy Whitmer.

"That's what I've got. I hope you find whoever killed Brett."

"Goodbye."

Thinking about Whitmer brought to mind the hiker at Feather Lake. We were at a pristine mountain lake, and he wanted to know how many reception bars my phone had. What was happening to people? I was beginning to wonder if we humans were falling into a collective trance. More and more I encountered people like that hiker and Whitmer. It was as if these screens we stare into were subtly, inexorably, sucking our humanity from us.

Four

I prepped hard for the boards, allowing myself afternoon walks along the shore of Fallen Leaf Lake. Encountering only a rare other hiker on the trail, the dark deep water spread a somberness. The wind delivered hushing sounds.

After pulling three all nighters, the next morning I rose early, dressed warmly and drove to where I could pull off near Sky Lake. A substantial perimeter encircled the blackened remains of Brett's house and garage; yellow police tape topped iron stakes pounded into the dirt. I slipped on surgical gloves and went to the two-story structure that housed the battery powered cart.

I unhooked heavy, unpainted wood shutters, leaned them against the side of the building. The screen had an aluminum frame. I worked it loose and tipped it against a shutter. The old double wood windows were difficult. At Sherman Investigations I'd learned how to grab where the upper and lower windows meet at the sash hook, and quickly jiggle the top window up and down about an eighth of an inch. On old windows, the hook would usually eventually vibrate away, unlocking them. It took work but the hook came free, and the lower window slid upward with a smooth purr, surely the result of Randy Zim's thorough maintenance. I crawled through, scooted onto the plywood counter, spun around, re-locked the windows and hopped down. I didn't bother with upstairs. Using my flashlight I examined downstairs as thoroughly as I would an ailing patient. Nothing had changed. I pushed open the wide back door, went outside; it locked automatically at closing. The screen and wood shutters were put back in place. I left too early to be caught by anyone coming to investigate the fires.

No way had Mr. Yellow Windbreaker driven a battery cart up from Lake Tahoe. He hadn't traversed tight and busy Highway 89 in it. Nobody would take that risk. And he didn't need to. He was the one who showed up at a crime scene. Did Stevens know more, or suspect more, than he was saying?

I kept to my studies as best I could. Mid afternoon, rather than walk at the lake I drove into South Lake Tahoe to my favorite guilty pleasure spot, Donut Hut, ordered hot chocolate and a cinnamon roll. I sat at the last empty brown Formica table that lined the shop's walls. At every other table one or two people looked at phones or laptops. The crowded room was quiet. I found an old copy of *Outside* magazine to thumb through. I decided to look into the death of the brother I'd never truly had. A guy whose parents took me in, and paid my way, during spring weekends while we played against elite high school basketball teams all over California. I'd known he was screwing up and hadn't tried to intervene. I'd laughed at the article I read about the exploits of Wild Man Boyd.

Estranged wife Elise Jansen's address was harder to find than most people's. Ninety percent can be found with simple internet searches. While her address didn't show easily, Elise Jansen, usually described as a super model, was all over the internet. I finally found a home address in El Dorado County property tax records. She lived amidst pines in a cul-de-sac off a long artery between Highway 89 and downtown South Lake Tahoe called Pioneer Trail. Elise Jansen's house was in a newer, upper middle-class section of wood houses stained one brown hue or another. Most vehicles were pickup trucks or bulky SUVs, made to endure long snowy winters.

Sitting on a wide cement driveway was a tired looking maroon Mercedes sedan that didn't go with the fine sprawling house that flowed back into forest. The house was chocolate brown. On the front door a steel knocker shone in the shape of a cross. I used it lightly. No answer. I gave it louder smacks, and heard movement inside.

A peep hole was utilized. A woman said, "If this is about a bill, I'm not paying it. Brett's debts were his own."

I said, "Elise? I'm a friend of Brett's. We kind of grew up together. I'm sorry about what happened."

The woman's voice was coarse, like someone who smoked and drank a lot. "Who exactly are you?"

"Jeff Taylor."

The door swung open. Elise's long blonde hair was a mess, as was her flowery robe. She stepped onto the porch and hugged me like I was a sailor returning home after years at sea. Her breath smelled distinctly of wine.

Elise shrieked, "You came! You came!"

Thinking a neighbor might see this, I unwrapped her arms from my middle. "May I come in?"

"Of course. You came."

Elise patted and shaped her hair as she led me into an ample home, as modern looking on the inside as it was woodsy on the outside. The living room walls displayed paintings large and small, bold abstracts and a few landscapes. Bronze sculptures topped two long low bookshelves, teak, polished. The décor was more Manhattan or Los Angeles than South Lake Tahoe.

Elise said, "Hey. Give me a chance to put myself together."

"Take your time."

Elise disappeared down a hallway. She looked to be just under six feet tall. A pair of beige slippers were left on a carpet of almost the same color. On a white tile counter separating the kitchen from the living room, an empty wine glass stood next to an empty wine bottle. I found a standing lamp, turned it on and checked out the books.

Elise returned wearing black skinny jeans and a lavender sweater that matched the color of her eyes. Her feet were bare. I sat in a corner chair upholstered in russet cloth. Elise sat on a glossy brown leather couch. She tucked her legs back behind her. In less than five minutes the disheveled woman who opened the door had transformed herself. She looked terrific. Yet Elise didn't look like she did in the internet pictures of her modeling one thing or another. In most of those she radiated an ethereal beauty. In person she simply looked classically attractive. I wondered if certain people blossom when photographed.

Elise smiled. It came quickly and vanished quickly. Looking at my mangled hand, in her coarse voice she said, "Ain't that a dog. What happened?"

"An accident. It's not worth talking about right now." I didn't know where to start. "My wife and I recently moved to Fallen Leaf Lake. A few days ago, I look at a newspaper headline, and there it is about Brett."

"You didn't come to see him?"

"I didn't know he lived here."

Elise looked outside through a sliding glass door. "Brett didn't know he was here half the time, either. That's what broke us up."

"Sorry to hear it."

Elise's lavender eyes went flat. "For three years we were on top of the world. We couldn't walk down a street without somebody taking our picture. He was all over, winning. I was modeling. We'd mesh schedules as best we could. These past couple years, after he quit skiing, have been hell."

I thought she might cry. She did not.

"What did you mean when you said, 'You came?'"

A wan smile. "Okay. I know it sounded weird."

Elise used both hands to lift the long blonde hair, which showed no dark roots, off the back of her lengthy neck. "Sometimes, when Brett gets—got—fongoed, he'd say, 'You watch. Jeff Taylor's going show up one day. We'll go down to the junior college and whip some youngsters on the court.' It was just drunk talk. But he repeated it so many times, when you said who you are, the words just came out. I'm. Well, I'm a mess."

"That's understandable."

Elise looked up. It was as if she were searching for someone.

"Even though I left him, Brett was still my guy. We talked on the phone most every day. We saw each other a couple times a week. I just couldn't live with him anymore. Too much drama."

Elise rose from the couch, shifted her body in the black skinny jeans and went to the kitchen. "You want some mineral water?"

"Yes, please."

"Jesus. You're like a Boy Scout. You read about Brett in the paper, find out where I live and come over to console me."

"There's more to it than that."

Through the kitchen counter opening I saw Elise grab two glasses. She took a plastic bottle from the refrigerator and filled the glasses. She returned, handed me water. She sat on the couch. She looked perplexed, confused.

"It's so strange you're here. I mean strange you came now. After Brett quit skiing, he became obsessed with that basketball team you both played on. Of course that was after he got hurt."

"That's why he quit? Because of injuries?"

"Because after he recovered, he never got his stuff back. When he finished eighth one week and tenth the next, he walked. He couldn't live with mediocrity. We drove back to Tahoe from Lake Tapawingo, Missouri, where there's a big tournament. He didn't talk the whole way. We finally get to Sky. First thing Brett does is take his skis behind the house. He goes to the garage, gets an axe. He chops the crap out of every ski."

Elise downed water. Somehow, it was an elegant act. "What do you want? You seem sincere. I'm not used to it. It makes me nervous."

"I want to find out if it was more than an overdose." I decided not to invite questions by mentioning cyanide. She'd find out soon enough. "If somebody killed Brett, I'm going to find him. I'm going to beat his brains out and turn him in. The Brett Boyd I knew was one of the greats."

Elise leaned back. She blinked a few times, registering my threat. "What about the police? They're not exactly ignoring it."

"The police don't feel guilty for not coming through for a childhood hero. I'd read about Wild Man Boyd." I brandished my half hand. "I know how quickly life can go south. I told myself I should contact him. Try to get him to slow down. Remember what counts. Obviously, I didn't."

Elise shuddered. Tears dripped. "For you, he might have slowed down." She lowered her head such that I couldn't see her face. "He ignored everybody else's warnings."

"It must be scary to go from being about the best in the world to an also ran."

Elise wiped her face, raised and set the shoulders high again. "What was scary was coming home after days on the road and finding Brett on the floor, moaning, saying he didn't want to live. I'd be up all night, worried he might hurt himself. In the morning, he'd act like nothing happened." Elise stood. She shook out the long hair. "Let yourself out. I need to be alone."

Elise walked down the hall again. She shut a bedroom door behind her. I checked out the classy living room and kitchen. Here was a model or former model, and there wasn't a personal photo to be seen in the well-choreographed space. That gained Elise Jansen points on my mental chalkboard.

Mail was scattered across a side table. Bills and advertisements. I found a pen in the side table drawer, and scrawled across the back of an envelope: *If you need anything call.* Then added my phone number and initials, and set the envelope against the empty wine bottle. I took a last look at the artsy house and closed the front door quietly behind me.

Back at The Lodge, I called Karen. Her steady voice was as clear as if she sat across from me.

"Hey Taylor. How goes it?"

I told Karen about visiting Elise. Her reaction to my arrival. Her words regarding Brett's telling her I'd show up someday.

I said, "What are your thoughts?"

"I can't wait till you get a job."

"But what's your gut tell you?"

"That if you don't pass the boards, you'll sleep alone for a year. When it's my turn to cook, you get dog food. That's for starters."

"I'll pass and you know it. I'm as ready as I'll ever be."

In my mind I saw Karen take her chestnut ponytail from between narrow shoulder blades, pull it around to in front, and nibble. When she did this it seemed to help her think.

Karen said, "Can't you be left alone without finding a way to complicate things?"

"I didn't do the complicating. Whoever killed Brett did the complicating."

Karen sighed. "This is your second call. You still haven't asked how my mom is."

"How's your mom doing? How's everybody doing?"

"You're too busy worrying about the tragedy of somebody you haven't seen in ten years to ask. Brett was a big part of your basketball life. I get it. I come back in a week and a half. Think you can remember to make it to the airport?"

"If you email me a reminder the day before."

"Taylor, I love you. But you're impossible."

"And inevitable."

This was our refrain.

Karen said, "Isn't that just a fancy way of saying I'm stuck with you?"

"I'm happy we understand each other."

Talking with Karen helped me see things in a new light. There was nothing I could do about Brett's death that would bring him back. My reflexive leap into trying to figure out what happened with him reflected guilt for not keeping in touch. I'd felt so sorry for myself about my wrecked hand that I deserted our friendship.

Darkness fell. I lit a fire with sticky pitch popping in Douglas fir logs. The granite fireplace was expansive enough I could stretch out on the hearth and have room to spare. I ate dinner and stuck to my studies. The phone rang. It showed Antonio as calling. When Karen and I helped out with his mom's ankle, we'd exchanged numbers.

"Hello, Antonio."

His words were fast. "A customer came in wearing those big sunglasses you said. Looks like he can cause trouble. He takes off the glasses, looks around and goes to the bar. I ask if he wants to look at a menu. He says, 'No way, Jose,' like it's funny or something."

"Keep an eye on him. I'll be in as fast as I can."

"How about I check the parking lot? Look in cars. If I see one with a yellow windbreaker inside, I'll get the license plate."

"Good idea. I'm on my way."

The road wound two dark miles from The Lodge to the highway, making it impossible to achieve much speed. It was another five miles to Antonio's. I passed the turn to Whitmer's house. At the restaurant I walked in looking straight ahead. The hostess welcomed me as "Dr. Jeff." Antonio appeared and motioned for me to follow him. We went to his tiny office. Antonio grabbed the white belt with both hands and hoisted it over his stomach.

"The man, he drinks in a hurry. He almost caught me looking in the cars. I hear the door make a scrape. I walk with my back to whoever came out until I hear an engine. I turn around. It was too far to see anything except it was a big SUV, not a truck. Dark colored."

"Thanks. You did what you could."

"We call my brother," Antonio said. "He lives pretty close. He can work the video. Have a seat."

I waited in the small office. A waiter brought a plate of nachos and a glass of water. I picked at the food. The waiter removed the plate and water glass. Then Antonio and Roberto entered. Roberto carried a small black box. A cable trailing it was clearly designed to plug into a computer.

Antonio said, "My brother, he knows this stuff. He set up the system."

Roberto took Antonio's chair. He sat, set the black metal box on the desk. He plugged it into Antonio's computer.

Roberto said, "My brother makes people happy. That is his gift." Roberto tapped keys. "I make people unhappy. That is my job."

Antonio said, "Please forgive. They will worry if I'm here long without explanation."

I sat with knees bumping against the small desk. Behind me, the door shut.

Roberto clicked away on Antonio's PC. He looked at Antonio's nail file, shook his head and put it in the top drawer of the desk. "My brother says, because of your hand, you have special powers."

"No. All I have is I never stop going after something important."

Roberto fast forwarded through the restaurant's video feed. He smiled in a way that reminded me of Antonio. Roberto made several clicks. "Here. Take a look."

I went around the desk and squeezed over to next to Roberto. He tilted the screen so I viewed at a better angle.

"First," Roberto said, "he comes in."

Roberto hit a key. On screen, in the low light of the restaurant, a man entered. The black-and-white image was grainy. Three steps in, he removed the oversized sunglasses. Roberto stopped the video. The man had a notable scar at his right eyebrow, about an inch long, and thick.

"It's not clear, but this might be your best look. Take your time."

"I can't say. I didn't get a good look at his face. Sunglasses covered that scar above his eye. I can't make a good guess at how tall he is, because when he stood, the cart's on wheels."

"I see." Roberto hit the start key. The guy took, one, two, three, four slow-motion steps. The whole way, his head swiveled back and forth. "To me," Roberto added, "he's looking for someone."

The video went to live speed as the man entered the bar, then froze.

"I get what you're saying. But how would he know to come here?"

"Everybody goes to Antonio's. Besides, he was here for less than ten minutes. Watch. From a different camera."

Roberto did the key tapping routine. The man left the bar. He glanced across the dining area. The last thing seen was him sliding on the humongous shades and reaching to open the restaurant door. Roberto stopped the video, giving me a profile of the man.

I said, "I don't know. I have no reason to think it's him except the sunglasses. Stevens with the police says all the security guys at Sky Lake Estates wear them. Couldn't it be a coincidence he comes here?"

"If he stayed a while, or ate something, yes. He slipped in and out in nine minutes, forty-six seconds. At that rate, he can check half the restaurants in town in one night."

"When it's not slow motion, he looks jumpy."

"Just so there's no misunderstanding. You want to know who he is. Right? I say this man wants to know who you are."

"He didn't get the best look at me, either. He was looking into the sun and facing a windstorm. He had on thick dark glasses. My sweatshirt hood was on."

Roberto said, "He doesn't need a good view of your face." Roberto raised his right hand. He wiggled it. "You've seen him. Maybe he thinks he should have acted right then, and he's trying to catch up."

"Acted?"

"I think you know what I mean."

Five

At returning to The Lodge, its post-summer isolation struck me. The road in from the highway dead-ended at three miles, with cabins lining much of the way. But after Labor Day few people were there. The closest year-round neighbor was half a mile away.

My thoughts returned to the conversation with Roberto. I told myself the odds were the guy who came into Antonio's wasn't the man who confronted me at Sky Lake. It could have been any of thousands of guys in the area. There was no solid reason to think the guy on camera was after me.

I didn't believe it for a second.

I tried to come to suppositions about Billy Whitmer. He didn't add up. He lets a stranger in his house, feeds me pizza and Diet Coke, praises Brett but expresses no feelings about Brett's death or the fires. There was an adolescent aura about him. From what I found online, Whitmer was a successful electrical contractor. Some of the jobs described on his site were complex. I wondered if they gave him satisfaction. I wondered how much he ingested of the drugs he sold on the side. In my head I heard the smooth radio voice that, upon reflection, reminded me of shopping mall music. Music that came and went and was never remembered.

I jumped out of the chair, spun around, looked toward the front door and realized the noise that jarred me was my phone jingling. The number on the phone didn't have a name attached to it. I looked through the dining room windows, to see if someone lurked outside.

"Hello."

"Jeff?"

"Yes."

"It's Elise Jansen. How are you tonight?"

"Just fine."

"Would you meet me for a drink?"

"Has something come up?"

"Jesus. Brett's dead. Jim Stevens called to warn me the papers are going to say the police think he was murdered. They found something suspicious in him." Elise cleared her throat. "I guess that qualifies as something coming up."

"Sorry. You caught me off guard."

"I haven't left this stupid house in three days. I need to go somewhere. I don't want to do it alone."

"I understand."

"Could you meet me in like half an hour? How about Mixx? The restaurant. You know it?"

"I've driven by. I'll be at the entrance."

Outside Mixx, rather than dusty SUVs and pickup trucks, low slung, polished cars lined the parking lot. An old fashioned green neon sign announced MIXX in slow, steady beats. Painted a mellow sea green with black window trimmings, the building stood out from its brown-stained neighbors. A brick walkway, under gabled olive-green canvas, led to the entrance. White Christmas lights were strung pole to pole. I walked toward the lights. The entrance door opened. Out came two glossy couples, laughing. Their teeth and faces shined. The men wore sports coats, dress shirts, dark slacks. The women wore dresses that would gain them entrance to exclusive nightclubs. I slid my hands into the kangaroo pocket of my gray Sacramento State sweatshirt.

A grimy Mercedes entered the lot. It joined my Subaru as two blotches among vehicles that cost more than most people's annual incomes. Elise stepped out of her car in a manner suggesting someone had opened the door for her. She spotted me, swung her long blonde hair and strode forward. Elise wore a short purple velvet dress with spaghetti straps, dark stockings and black heels that rose her to as tall as my six-three. On arrival, she looked me over, jeans, tennis shoes and the sweatshirt.

"I wasn't thinking. I should have warned you." She shivered against the chilly night.

"Will they let me in?"

Elise took my arm. "They'll let us in."

Inside, a young woman, cheeks glistening, long black hair riding high in a complicated maneuver, greeted Elise as Mrs. Boyd. They exchanged fluttery cheek kisses.

The hostess said, "A party agreed to switch tables. They were gracious about it."

"Send them Dom Perignon on ice. Thank you, Maryanne."

"Of course."

We followed Maryanne to a back corner of the restaurant. People looked up, table after table, at towering Elise Jansen.

I pulled out a chair for her. As the chair slid forward beneath her, Elise smoothed a hand down the back of her short dress. I took the chair across from her, which backed to the wall of the restaurant. The wall was painted a fainter sea green than the exterior. People's heads went up and down—looking and then not looking at Elise—as if bobbing for apples.

Hostess Maryanne said, "Mrs. Boyd?"

Elise raised two fingers.

Maryanne turned to me. "Is that okay with you, sir?"

"I like surprises."

Maryanne walked away. Everything, as well as everyone in the room, gave off a clean sheen. This was not the laid back South Lake Tahoe of down jackets and flannel shirts I knew.

Elise said, "Thank you for coming. If I came in alone, everybody would be staring."

I didn't know her well enough to know if she were joking.

"These folks probably think I'm your handyman. Spent the afternoon cleaning your rain gutters."

"More honorable work than most of the people in here do."

I was warming to Elise.

A short, slim, dapper man with a trim silver goatee, wearing a buttoned white coat and red bow tie, wheeled forth a silver cart bearing two cocktail glasses. At arrival he gave us each a partial bow.

"Good evening, Mrs. Boyd."

They exchanged a thank you and a you're welcome. The man set a thin-stemmed cocktail glass in front of Elise, then one in front of me. He bowed, and left, pushing the silver cart past people who watched him with curiosity.

I said, "What is this, 1957?"

Elise said, "Kind of. That's why I let them call me Mrs. Boyd. It fits the restaurant, the whole place."

Elise took a swallow of her drink. "No one ever bothers me here. When Brett and I were, you know, rolling, this was the only place we could go and were rarely asked for autographs." She lifted her cocktail glass. "Gin gimlets, by the way."

"I had no idea Brett married a famous model."

"Used to be."

"Retired?"

Elise shook her head. "Half retired. I cut way back the past couple years. I took the most jobs from May to September, when people could check in on Brett. When winter came, I stayed put. It was like living in a foxhole. If someone dropped by, Brett told him to go away."

We settled into small talk. At her asking, I retold the story of losing half of my hand for what seemed the thousandth time. I'd told it so many times I didn't really hear the words anymore.

Elise said, "You haven't asked, but I'll tell you. I met Brett at a party in Malibu. When we talked it felt like we drifted above the whole scene. Like we were a separate entity. It was great but spooky. It was like we didn't choose. We were together and that was that."

Elise flashed two fingers. She didn't look to see if anyone noticed. She moved her body in a way that indicated she crossed her legs. "It's so weird you're here. After all these years."

"Maybe it's not a coincidence."

"Are you saying you think it's fate?"

"Something like that. I don't have an organized set of beliefs. I just know there's more to life than biology."

The man with the silver goatee wheeled forth gimlets. I told him that would be my last. Elise downed a third of the cocktail in a gulp.

I said, "How are Brett's parents taking things?"

"Or not. When Brett went off the rails, his parents pretty much disowned him. He was the golden boy who turned into mud. They blamed me. They were right. Instead of Brett coming home for down time during the holidays, we'd go to Berlin. Berlin seduced us. The galleries, the shops, the sophistication of the people. Have you been?"

"I've never been to Europe."

Elise looked at me like she couldn't fathom someone hadn't been to Europe. "For real?"

"I'll get there someday."

She finished her drink. She raised one tapered finger.

Elise said, "You're not interested in me."

"Of course I am."

"I mean you're not going to hit on me. I can tell."

"That's right."

Elise swung her hair. "God that's refreshing."

"Even married, guys still come on to you?"

"Duh. But it only got bad after Brett was a mess. Jim, with the police? Even he started getting friendlier when Brett got out of hand. Since it happened, he finds an excuse to call every day. Do you know who he is?"

I said we'd met, went to Sky Lake and looked things over. I told Elise about the man in the yellow windbreaker, how he came on aggressively when I walked toward their chalet. Their now burned-down chalet and garage. I did not mention the pistol. I told her Stevens' explanation about the oversized sunglasses.

"I'm sure he's right. Jim knows everybody." Elise gestured in a slightly awkward way that indicated the drinks were affecting her. "If things got way, way out of hand, I'd call Jim."

It seemed the bartender had stocked a queue of gimlets in anticipation of Elise's arrival, because round number three was already rolling our way. The man with the silver goatee did not smile nor frown. Elise's cocktail glass was efficiently removed, and replaced. A glass of water, no ice, was set in front of me. The man bowed and wheeled away the silver cart.

Elise took a sip. She pursed her lips, tasting gin. "A couple times when I was gone, working, Brett went nuts and started breaking things. Somebody would call Jim. Jim would wrestle him down,

50

handcuff him to the bed and wait Brett out. He was a huge help." Elise took a quick sip. Her words came faster. "Jim says Brett would say he wanted to die, but if he killed himself the insurance wouldn't pay. Because of the size of the policy, and the company's looking into Brett's history, they'd only issue a policy with a no suicide clause."

"You lost me with 'the insurance.'"

"Sorry. I forget we just met. Of course you wouldn't know. Everything's still swirling on me." Elise brushed her hair back. She reset her bare shoulders. "When we were raking it in, Brett took out a life insurance policy for eight hundred grand. He spent hella lot of time driving all over the country, towing a trailer with his gear. He said sooner or later there'd be a wreck. I had to provide payments the last couple years."

Elise raised a tapered finger. Then she reached across and flicked it against my water glass. "Don't worry. Four's the limit. House rules for Mrs. Boyd."

A woman about my age, in the same white getup and red bow tie as the drink-delivering man with a silver goatee, walked to a black Steinway grand piano. Light applause tinkled across the room.

Elise smiled. "Here comes your 1957."

The woman played Sinatra songs, some Cole Porter and Irving Berlin. The lavender-blue in Elise's eyes grew soft. Without speaking she stood and started for the exit. Her steps were off balance. I caught up with her; Elise took my arm. Outside, the air braced me. At reaching her car, I insisted on following Elise home. That she flicked the lights on and off once she was safely inside.

"Whatever you say, Boy Scout."

Six

I pulled into the wide, three-sided carport at The Lodge, next to Karen's dusky orange Volvo, and cut the headlights. My phone jingled. No name. It wasn't Elise because I'd put her name and number in my contacts list. Noting how thoroughly dark it was in those woods at night—I'd need my little flashlight to make it to the front door—I tapped and said hello.

"Jeff? Roberto here. Sorry if I woke you."

"You didn't."

"I didn't want to wait till tomorrow with this. I just got a call from Luisa. She works the entrance lobby, swing shift. A man came up and asked if a guy with a hand like yours came in. He said he borrowed fifty bucks from this man last night. Promised to pay him back tonight at ten. He said the man with the hand was six-two or six-three, thirty to thirty-five, thinning brown hair."

"What did Luisa say?"

"Nothing. She hasn't seen you, and she wouldn't, anyway. Louisa says even inside the lobby he wore wrap-around shades, biggest ones she's ever seen."

"Did he mention my name?"

"Even though Luisa told him she hadn't seen anybody who matched your description, he still asked for your name. Real quick, like he was trying to trick her. No, he doesn't know your name."

"I saw him with the Blizzard windbreaker on. It makes sense he'd go there, to check if I had."

Roberto said, "I train my people to see things somebody's hiding. Louisa says when he walked out, she saw a bulge under his sweater at the back waist band. She went outside and was ready to take pictures of his vehicle if he came out of the pay lot. But he walked fast down the street. She couldn't leave work to follow. Luisa says he looks like he's cranked up on something."

"Anymore good news?"

A loud rattling, then a clanging sound shot from in front of the large dark house. I threw open the car door and shouted, "Who's there! Come on, who's there!" I grabbed the flashlight from the cup holder between the front seats.

Roberto said, "What the hell is that?"

I snapped on the flashlight. My adrenaline zinged like fishing line spooling out of a reel while a big fish fights for its life. Again the sound, like metal. I shined the light toward the sound. Ignoring me, a raccoon continued trying to pry off the lid I'd tied down with wire on the metal garbage can. The raccoon worked furiously. I waved the light back-and-forth. It froze.

Roberto said, "Goddamn it, what's going on?"

"It's just a raccoon. I couldn't see. Give me a minute, I'll go inside."

I left the raccoon to wrestle with the metal can, locked the Subaru and entered the house. I made a mental note to take the garbage to the neighborhood dumpster out by the highway. I switched on lights, locked the door behind me. My red switchblade waited on a pine coffee table.

I sat. "Sorry. The noise scared me. Where were we?"

"I was about to suggest you go to South Lake Tahoe police tomorrow. Don't call. They'll fill out a form. It will disappear. Ask for Sergeant Stevens."

"Why him? Besides, Blizzard's Nevada. He's California."

"Boyd's death, or murder, was California. Nevada police won't be interested. Trust me on this. Tell Jim I saw your guy with a gun in his waistband. He rushed away down the sidewalk. I didn't go after him because I didn't want to risk an incident in the crowded street. Tell him me, not Luisa."

"But that's not true. I was told to never lie to the police."

"What are you, a Boy Scout?"

"Apparently so."

Sleep didn't come easily. Every outdoor noise woke me. Awake, I heard more noises. Raccoons, bears, possums, skunks, branches cracking in wind? Something human caused? The man in the yellow windbreaker coming after me? I assumed he'd killed Brett. Since I'd seen him at the scene the day after Brett's body was found, and he was now popping up looking for me, it was reasonable to think he wanted to put me down as well.

In the morning, bleary-eyed, I pulled into the rock-walled South Lake Tahoe police station at eight sharp. I went through the metal detector and was walked down the hall I'd been led down before. I knocked on the open door of the office. The woman officer was not there. Stevens was, tapping on a keyboard, eyes glued to a computer screen. The other officer did the same at his desk.

I said, "Could I speak with you about something?"

Stevens did not stand. "I'm listening."

The other officer caught the standoffish reception. He said, "I'm listening."

I entered the room. Neither officer moved. Their eyes stayed on computer screens.

I said, "I need to talk to you about developments in the case."

"What case is that?"

"I know we got off to a bad start. I can't change that. But you should know about the guy who confronted me at Sky Lake."

"That again?"

I recounted the man's appearing at Antonio's. Soon as I mentioned Roberto, and looking at video footage with him, Stevens raised his right hand. He told me to stop. He looked to the younger officer.

"Take this down. Tell him if he needs to go slower. Mr. Taylor seems a bit wound up this morning."

The younger man in blue, who was in sync with Stevens' marine haircut and lean frame, typed something on his keyboard. "Okay."

I described what was on the security camera in Antonio's, and what Roberto told me had occurred at Blizzard Casino. This earned two small nods of Stevens' chin.

He said, "Okay, I hear you. What do you expect us to do? Give you protection? There's no proof this is the same person you saw at Sky. Even if it is the same person, he doesn't know you from Adam."

I flashed my trashed hand. "Sooner or later, he'll find me."

Stevens seemed to think this over. "Possible."

I was steaming, and trying not to let it show. "Thank you for your time." I headed for the doorway.

From behind me I heard, "Let me see you out."

Stevens popped up and headed after me. He caught up just before the glass exit doors opened automatically. Without our speaking, he accompanied me to my car. Stevens stepped ahead and pressed a hand against the driver's door.

His cheeks sprouted red spots. "I want to talk to you about Elise Jansen."

"What about her?"

"She's vulnerable right now. Anything someone says could be

taken to an extreme. It can get amplified in her mind. I called to check on her yesterday afternoon. She was crying. She said you'd come over."

"Brett and I went way back. Of course my visit upset her."

We were not two feet apart.

Stevens said, "Don't fill her head with unconfirmed speculations. Do I make myself clear?"

"Give me an example."

"I've done my research. You managed to insert yourself into the investigation of a state senator. People got killed. You inserted yourself into the death of an elderly man not related to you, and caused a ruckus. I'm telling you, stay out of Elise's life."

"Is that because of the money you know she's about to come into? Or is it because you see me like the guy in the windbreaker, who you say was driving around looking to poke his nose into anything he could find?"

"It's because Elise is a good girl. Don't make things unnecessarily difficult for her."

"Elise is more than a good *girl*. She stuck by my friend when he was a mess," I said. "Goodbye. I gave you potential info on Brett's killer. I hope it helps."

I looked to his hand pressed against the driver's door. Stevens removed it. I got in the car and drove away.

Seven

I headed toward Fallen Leaf Lake. My phone sang its tune. In glowing letters: Whitmer.

"Hello."

That mellifluous radio voice: "I've just concluded an appointment that will be of interest to you."

"You mean you're not out working hard this morning?"

"I made an exception. He's a regular."

"What's his pleasure?"

"All you need to know is, he's wearing a yellow windbreaker with the word security on an arm. Looks like he can handle himself. He's probably still at Ralston Beach. He always takes a walk, to make it look legit. You learn anything new?"

"No time. I've been studying like hell for the state medical exams."

"Like becoming a doctor?"

"That's the goal."

"Just think, you'll be able to write prescriptions."

"In your dreams."

"I'd hate to lose a regular, but if this is the guy, he should go down."

Ralston Beach was a mile off the highway, half a dozen miles north of town. Packed every day in summer, to get in you waited for vehicles to leave one at a time. After Labor Day weekend, however, it was sparsely populated. People let their dogs, yapping joyfully, chase floating balls into the cold lake. The sandy tan beach, clean and smooth, afforded a panoramic view of Lake Tahoe. Small waves nipped at the shore. They made delicate hissing sounds. The man in question walked southward. Accompanying him, on his left, a leashed German Shepherd. The dog seemed to prance. The yellow windbreaker reflected sunlight. I broke into a jog.

There seemed no safer place to confront the man who had confronted me at Sky Lake. We were in open space with people around. I picked up my pace. The man had no idea I was coming up behind him. He had ample shoulders. Even hunched a bit, walking in wind, he exuded strength.

Passing him, I looked over and said, "Good morning."

Roberto Ramirez. His smile came instantly. He halted; the dog sat tall, its tongue wagging, its eyes on me. I stopped running and acted like I needed to catch my breath.

Roberto said, "Rocky, say hi to Dr. Jeff."

Three distinct barks, followed by sitting still. The barks carried the promise of strength and discipline.

Roberto said, "What a nice surprise."

No way was he as surprised as I was. We shook hands amiably.

"I was told this is a good place to run. The sand gives the legs a workout."

Roberto tugged the windbreaker away from his body. "Like I said, these turn up everywhere. It's free advertisement for the casino."

"You come here often?"

"Every chance I get. I'm in that cave ten to seven, six days a week. In January I get nights again. For now, this is my me time."

Roberto pointed out the casinos miles away at Stateline. At that distance, they shimmered. He named them, one by one, ending with Blizzard, which appeared turquoise under morning sun.

Roberto asked the time. When I told him the time he acted surprised, and said he was going to be late for work.

"I better let you get back to your run. Good to see you."

"You, too." I broke into a jog and waved overhead.

Roberto didn't ask about the man who badgered me at Sky Lake. The same man who later showed up at the casino with a pistol tucked in the back waist of his pants, who Roberto suggested might be looking to kill me. Roberto obviously had other things on his mind.

I ran to the end of the long squishy beach. Walking back, I texted Whitmer: *Wrong guy. Thanks for trying.*

The return: *Happy to help.*

Life settled into studying, lunch, an afternoon hike at Fallen Leaf Lake, then dinner and studying until the words blurred. I did wonder about Roberto Ramirez and Billy Whitmer.

Elise called to invite me to a small gathering, noon the next day, in a banquet room behind the bar at Mixx.

"There'll only be about ten of us. I don't want a funeral, but some of us who knew Brett should get together. You know, a celebration of life."

"Will Brett's parents be there?"

"I invited them. They declined, which was a relief."

"Frank Baumer and Stevens?"

"Frank never really approved of me. Like my world was a bad influence on Brett. Compared to Brett I'm a straight arrow."

"Stevens?"

"Didn't invite him. He's a little too friendly. Will you come? Tell people what Brett was like as a kid?"

"Of course I'll come."

The next day I put on what I thought of as my wedding and funeral clothes, a dark sports coat, pale blue Arrow shirt, black slacks. I polished my brown dress shoes. White-tipped rain clouds led me south toward town. I fiddled with the radio and found a classical music station playing the haunting piano music of Erik Satie. It was like having a private service for Brett in the moving car. Individual notes sounded with faultless clarity. Trees lining the highway were still, like mourners.

The parking lot at Mixx was at most a quarter full. Mixx was more a dinner and evening drinks place. Elise's dirty Mercedes sat toward the front of the lot, among a couple of what looked like freshly washed rental cars and two pickup trucks. I parked at the back left edge, alongside the trees. I didn't want to leave the gathering and end up walking with Elise. My mood was not in tune with celebrating a life. I was there out of respect for Brett and a sense of duty.

Maryanne, of a couple nights before, welcomed me with a brilliant smile. "Come on back."

We passed mostly empty tables, went through the bar to a banquet room. It smelled sweet. A small section had three round tables set with cloth napkins and sparkling restaurant silverware.

At seeing me, Elise waved. "So glad you came!" Three women surrounded her, tall, slim, and dressed in black dresses hemmed just above their knees. A fourth woman, a couple of decades older than the others, stocky, stood a bit to the side. She wore a black-and-red pin-striped business suit. At the base of her neck, gold-framed glasses hung from a gold chain. Elise wore a dark pants suit. She glowed such that I assumed she'd had a libation or two before going to Mixx.

Against the back wall were tables with a fine buffet laid out on white tablecloths. A youngish couple, in jeans and cowboy boots, inched their way down the food line. A middle-aged couple was ahead of them. The man wore a crisp white shirt that matched the white of his mustache. He had a gray ponytail pulled through a red rubber band. Both women looked like they could toss down whiskey.

Elise introduced me to her model friends. Each gave me perky double cheek kisses. All three were trim without curves, with shiny hair and perfect skin. Perhaps they'd conferred on perfume as they smelled the same. The atmosphere seemed less than real.

The woman with dangling glasses stepped to me. Hair dyed the color of a freshly minted penny, school-girl bangs dyed cotton candy pink, she said, "Annabee Flowers."

Elise flashed a jumbo smile. "Annabee's my agent. We've been together like forever."

We shook. Annabee squeezed my half hand hard, no holding back like most people do. "I don't have a date. Neither do you. Assist me in selecting lunch."

That was okay with me. The bouncy twiggy women looked ready to parade up and down the banquet room at any appearance of a camera. I couldn't imagine conversing with them.

At reaching the food tables, I handed Annabee a white plate. We duplicated the couple ahead of us, sliding along, plucking veggies, wraps, tiny triangle sandwiches stuck through with toothpicks.

Staring at a mound of shrimp, in a low voice Annabee said, "Straight talk. How's she holding up?"

"As well as can be expected. Though I don't really know her."

"Elise said you're one of Brett's oldest friends."

"It's a long story."

"We don't have time for long. Tell me what you think."

"With an emphasis on think, not know, it seems even though they'd been living apart, Elise loved Brett with all her heart."

"She gave up fame and fortune for him. But I got to say, before he went to pot, pun intended, he was a major-league catch." Annabee set down her filled plate. She lifted her glasses, set them on her nose and looked at me. Her glasses made her greenish-blue eyes appear like I was looking through a magnifying glass. "Don't let her go down Brett's river. Once you get in too deep, it's inevitable you drown." Her voice still low, Annabee said, "Promise?"

"I can't. This is only the third time I've seen Elise. In total, we haven't spent three hours together."

Annabee looked up, winced. She whispered, "Do you think somebody killed him?"

This brought over-the-shoulder looks from the couple ahead of us.

"I don't know." A convenient lie. "It could turn out either way."

Annabee removed the glasses; they chimed against the golden chain. We took a table. The gray-haired couple sat at the next table over. They introduced themselves and said they were Elise's neighbors. Keeping my hands below the table's edge, I introduced myself as a high school friend of Brett's. Remembering Brett as the leader of that all-star team, waves of heat washed through me. I remembered Brett teaching us, like a coach, without ever acting superior. My chest tightened. I looked around, thinking I'd been at that strange gathering before. Everything grew increasingly familiar. I experienced déjà vu, with every moment remembered, one after another. Heat emanated off my body. I wiped my forehead with a cloth napkin. I swallowed as if forcing something down a sore throat.

I turned to Annabee. "Excuse me."

I made my way to Elise. She looked at me as if sobering up. "What is it?"

"I feel dizzy. I'm going for some air. I won't be long."

Just out the door, I saw a black Range Rover, engine thrumming, near the clump of vehicles that included Elise's run-down Mercedes. A person in the driver's seat clicked photos. I stayed under the shade of the walkway canopy, which meant I didn't get a look at the driver. I thought male as the person's hair seemed short. The Range Rover circled around to the right, and was gone. All I'd gleaned was someone driving a black Range Rover and the license plate was California.

I ran to my car. Vehicles raced past on the highway. I pulled into southbound traffic. If I got lucky I'd see the Range Rover turn onto a residential street. I could come back later and look for it, get its license plate number. Clint Sherman would get me the name and address of the owner in minutes.

I wasn't lucky. Leaving town I passed a golf course and drove into the dispiriting burned edge of the Kamen Fire of two years prior, a quarter million acres roasted. The Range Rover turned left toward Luther Pass. Two other cars made the turn ahead of me. The road climbed through the depressing burn scar. All at once the beauty of the region was with me again. Mountains, evergreens, granite boulders. Then over the pass and down, looking at a valley with the West Fork of the Carson River a gray ribbon meandering through its heart. At the confluence with Highway 88, the Range Rover turned right. The next car went left. Before I reached Highway 88, the other car turned right. I stayed at the stop sign until the Range Rover's driver couldn't see me in the rear-view mirror. I turned right. A mile later the car in front of me turned onto a driveway. Ahead, the black Range Rover.

I stayed far back. I slowly crested Carson Pass. Snaking down, Caples Lake was to the left, a cold navy-blue beauty. The road straightened. The Range Rover pulled into the center turn lane at a road leading to Kirkwood Ski Resort. There was no oncoming traffic.

With no one behind me, I slowed to a crawl. The vehicle didn't turn into Kirkwood. It spurted ahead and turned right onto a road I'd never been on or even noticed. I followed, keeping well back.

I passed a sign: *No Services 31 Miles*. Again I entered the Kamen Fire scar, turn after turn through ravaged forest, lonely land. One car passed the other direction. A few miles later, on the right, a sign so weathered the letters were barely readable: *Landauer Ski Resort*. Passing it I saw the Range Rover parked in open space. With no traffic I easily flipped a U-turn, crossed the road and stopped on the shoulder, engine running, facing the wrong direction.

The black SUV sat in the middle of a wide flat dirt plane littered with the remains of deserted structures. Some sat alone, untouched by the Kamen wildfire yet vandalized years before. A badly burned hotel was the largest building. It seemed every window in every building was shattered. Skeleton ski lifts of charred poles rose up slopes at opposite ends of the desolate valley. A few ghostly chair lifts remained, suspended in air. Nothing moved.

Was he daring me to enter? Of course he was. No smoke came from the SUV's tailpipe. I lowered the window, grabbed binoculars. I searched for but didn't see a driver. Long abandoned Landauer Ski Resort looked like photos you see of villages bombed in war. It seemed there was little space between the bare lonely ground and low gray clouds. Through the open window came nothing but a feeling of emptiness.

I wanted to confront the man I believed killed Brett. I wanted to pummel him. Growing up in an isolated town, you develop tribal identity. Anyone who damages a member of your tribe, even if he's not your friend, must be damaged equally. Though he grew up in a different small town, Brett had been an integral part of my personal tribe. It never occurred to me to follow norms or the law.

The driver had parked such that I'd have to go into the

dilapidated ski resort and behind the vehicle to see its license plate. The front plate was missing. That wouldn't be accidental. I took out my phone, brought it to my eyes.

A resounding shot broke the silence. The shot came from one of the ghost town buildings.

Another shot split thin mountain air. The Subaru's frame shifted as if hit by a burst of wind. I slammed the car into drive, stomped the gas pedal and ducked. My sight line barely above the dashboard, the world reeled by like a herky-jerky cartoon. If I made it to Highway 88 there would be people around. I drove fast but not so fast I'd lose control on a curve. All the way over Carson Pass on Highway 88 and then over Luther Pass on Highway 89, I did not see the black Range Rover in the rear-view mirror.

I pulled into a gas station at Meyers, an unincorporated stretch of highway a few miles before South Lake Tahoe. I parked in back, walked to the side and watched traffic. No black Ranger Rover missing a front plate. This did not surprise me.

What did surprise me was the bullet hole in my left front fender. Inches in front of the tire. I figured angling downward because not a mark could be found elsewhere on the car. The guy was clearly an expert marksman. He could easily have taken me out.

While working for Clint Sherman I'd been tutored on how to tail people. Zeke Tillman respected traditions. He wore a white shirt, tie and tie clasp and slacks, no matter the Sacramento heat. His language peppered with curse words, his face was a puffy red, his eyes perpetually swollen like he'd just woken up. At Clint's instruction, for a month I'd ridden shotgun with him. Zeke was the company specialist in tail jobs.

I'd been reckless, careless. Dumb. I'd revealed myself to the target at the turn off to Kirkwood. Obsessed with finding Brett's killer, I was not entirely of sound mind.

In South Lake Tahoe I passed Mixx restaurant without stopping. I sure as hell didn't want to go in and explain my absence from the gathering by saying I'd followed the man I believed murdered Brett.

With no witnesses around why didn't the yellow windbreaker man shoot me?

Eight

My attempts to study were thirty-minute stints, interspersed with internet searches regarding Brett and Elise. First I looked for hints Brett had enemies. A heated rivalry? Regarding Elise, her career took off about the time she turned twenty-one and stayed at high altitude until Brett quit water skiing. I found no examples of her feuding with anyone in the fashion industry.

Annabee was right. Elise gave up the big-time for an erratic life with Brett.

Chronologically, material about Brett almost disappeared online, with the exception of his surprising third place finish in the Cal Ski/Ski competition the previous April.

I called Elise.

She picked up. "Goddamn you. You embarrassed me. Annabee goes out to look for you. You're nowhere to be found."

"I know. But I have to talk to you about something. Something serious. Can you talk privately? Are they all gone?"

Elise's words slurred. "Annabee's staying over. She's out for the night. She took something. The mods are in the air."

"Mods?"

"Models. There's a New York show this weekend. They're in the air right now. I have to drive Annabee to the airport hella early. She volunteered to stay over, so I won't be alone." The repeating of things, and the slurring, told me Elise had been drinking heavily. "Sir-urs-ly, Jeff. You hurt my feelings."

I recounted the man snapping photos outside of Mixx, and following the black Range Rover to Kirkwood. I skipped the gunshots at Landauer Ski Resort. I said I'd thought it would be easier for her if I didn't pop back into the gathering after an absence of more than an hour. She'd want an explanation. Giving one in front of those people was impossible. When I finished, the airwave fell silent.

Elise said, "Am I in danger?"

"It's me he's looking for. I know that one hundred percent."

Of course it was possible Elise was in danger. This wasn't the time to venture into the subject.

She slurred, "Does all this mean, for-real, Brett was murdered?"

"More likely than not."

I heard what sounded like the clink of glass hitting a solid surface. Elise cleared her throat. "How did he know to go to Mixx?"

"My best guess, and it's only a guess, is he got your address and followed you. He waited a while, to be sure no more cars parked by yours. He wanted to get pictures of all the license plates."

"Shit."

I got up from a wicker chair and went to the granite hearth. I'd been too preoccupied to remember to light a fire. That told me I was shaken by the guy in the black Range Rover. If I hadn't parked far off to the side, he'd have my license plate number. Maybe he got it at the ski resort. I tried to picture the man. Mostly I conjured thick wrap-around sunglasses and an arrogant grin. Solid, agitated. Wearing doe-skin gloves. No mustache or beard, nor other distinguishing feature except the scar I later saw at his right eyebrow.

Elise said, "You still there?"

"I'm trying to remember what he looked like, at Sky Lake."

Elise said, "You know what? That was weird today. I'm no longer part of their world. The mods, the clothes. The endless traveling. I don't talk their talk. I think Annabee only keeps me on because I didn't leave when Storm Talent tried to poach me."

"And for her commission, when you take a job."

"Jeff, you've turned a weird day into a sleepless night."

I ran my bad hand across the soot-stained granite. It felt good to experience rubbing sensations in the finger stubs, to remind me they were more than ludicrous stumps. I said, "It's only right to tell you what I know."

I'd told Elise less than half of what I knew.

She took a swallow of whatever she was drinking. Elise said, "I'm scared. I take Annabee to the airport, then I'm alone. I never realized I counted on Brett like he counted on me."

I walked to the square wood windows that, during daytime, looked out and down upon dark Fallen Leaf Lake. Light from inside splashed across the trunks of pine trees. Beyond that, blackness. "I hope you can get some sleep."

Elise said, "Don't worry about me. Modeling gives you alligator thick skin. By the way, the girls think your hand is cool. They talked about it like it's an accessory. These were my best friends?"

Thinking life had been harder for Brett and Elise than for me, I said, "Goodnight. You'll get through this."

"I always do."

Elise hung up.

Besides not lighting a fire, I hadn't thought to eat. I didn't like it that the guy in the Range Rover probably knew Elise's car and home address.

I called Karen. I made sure to ask after her mom.

She said, "You're a lousy fake. You're still wrapped up in what may have happened to Brett. I bet you didn't remember it's three hours later here. I was just about to go to bed."

"Guilty. Let's start with your day. Then I'll tell you about my strange one."

We talked for half an hour.

I called Sergeant Stevens. No answer; I left a message, requesting he call me. My phone sounded in less than five minutes. I told Stevens about what I'd seen in the parking lot at Mixx, and following the Range Rover. I didn't mention Roberto and Billy Whitmer. Unlike with Elise, I told Stevens about the gunshots at the former ski resort.

Stevens said, "I told you to stay away from Elise. How was I unclear?"

"She contacted me. She asked me to tell those at the gathering what Brett was like when we were kids. Besides, where I go or don't go is none of your damn business."

No response. I pictured Stevens, the gray buzz cut, the cowlick, a hand adjusting black rectangular glasses. I pictured anger owning his face.

I said, "If nothing else, you have the type and color of what the guy who harassed me at Sky Lake drives. The guy who later shows up at the restaurant Antonio's, then Blizzard Casino."

Stevens said, "I wrote it down. Goodbye."

Elise called the next morning. "Ever been to Cradle Lake?"

"I've only seen it on a map."

"After this weekend, the road up there is closed till May. This is our last chance for the year."

The *our* made me uneasy. I both wanted not to become a frequent friend to troubled Elise, and wanted to give her care, make sure she didn't head down that river Annabee Flowers described. My mentor in medical school, Dr. Fisher, told me the starting point to becoming a good physician is to put other people ahead of oneself.

I said, "Are you doing okay?"

"Actually, yes. After seeing Annabee off, I had a good cry. The two hours type. I stretched and did Pilates. It helped get my head straight. Come by my place at noon and I'll show you a good time."

My heart hopped. I didn't speak.

Elise broke into coarse laughter. "You're one gullible Boy Scout. See you at noon. If you're a vegetarian, speak up now."

I returned to studying. When driving to Elise's I found I was a tad excited, and felt guilty because of Karen and creepy because Elise was Brett's wife. She emerged from her house beaming. In both hands were white shopping bags with handles. Her mass of blonde locks moved up and down with each step. I motioned for Elise to put the bags in back. Not getting out to help was part of not wanting to grow too chummy. Elise climbed in, shut the door. She leaned across the front seat and blew on my face.

"Smell that?"

"Spearmint?"

"No. No alcohol."

I shifted into drive. "And to think it's ten after twelve. That's quite an accomplishment."

"Hey. I went to town and bought us lunch. Can't you give me a break?"

"I shouldn't have said that."

I drove to the highway, headed east and then south into evergreen forest. Elise gave directions though said nothing more; my smart-ass crack had hurt her feelings. That told me she knew her drinking was a problem. Good. A couple of turns and we joined a tight road with a log gate tied back parallel to unkempt pavement.

The road was littered with potholes. I maneuvered around them. We climbed to a ridge with view of neighboring mountains. The day was warm, the air laced with the smell of pine and cedar trees.

I parked under tree shadow, reached into the backseat for binoculars. I got out of the car and scanned the sunny stretches of the twisty road below.

Elise climbed out and stood next to me. "I don't get it."

"If we're being followed, we'll see him five minutes before he gets here. We cut downhill through the trees, hook up with any number of trails and get to the store at Fallen Leaf. On the way I call Stevens. There's only one way in, one way out. If the police catch the guy up here, they'll get his ID. Who knows what else."

"You mean you didn't come for lunch and hanging out?"

"Let's call it fifty-fifty." I kept watch on the road below.

Elise tugged the sleeve of my sweatshirt. "I need a rest from thinking about Brett. And being scared. For today, can we not talk about that stuff?"

"If the suspect doesn't show, not a problem."

I watched the road for a dozen minutes. Elise grew impatient, paced uphill and back, and fell into some kind of stretching routine. We headed out again. We reached a parking lot blocked by the same log-style gate that was still open at the beginning of the road. I parked. We each took a shopping bag and hiked up a trail of dirt and crunchy grit. Climbing, it seemed like you could reach your hand into the sky's perfect blue. Half a mile later Cradle Lake came into view. A bowl of snow-melt water. Shingled cabins stood back from shore. The cabins were separated by tall green trees and granite boulders. The trail curved right. Over a hump of ground and we reached the lake. The cabins, boarded up till spring, were behind us. A small store and office were also boarded up. Painted black on a piece of plywood: *See you May 22!*

On the other side of the lake, a granite cliff rose sharply. Between us and the high cliff, a sandy beach basked under warm sun. Elise led the way. Miles from other people, moving past trees across lumpy sand, she walked with the same standing-tall confidence of a runway excursion. Elise walked like she owned the place.

One of the large shopping bags contained a brown blanket. Elise opened the blanket, smoothed it over sand, and sat. She gestured toward the lake. "This is all ours."

She unlaced brown hiking boots, worked them off her feet. Her socks were a pale green. Her oat-colored sweater outlined a sumptuous figure. Elise didn't fit the cliché of a toothpick-skinny model.

I said, "This is stunning."

To the left of the cliff, granite boulders the size of automobiles lined water's edge and were stacked all the way back over a granite hillside. The stone backdrop blocked wind. Elise plucked two green bottles of Pellegrino water, turkey wraps, two half pints of sautéed veggies and one of potato salad. She passed the potato salad to me.

"If I weigh more than one-thirty-five, they'll put me out to pasture."

The lake's water scarcely moved.

We ate. When finished, Elise grinned like a teenager and produced a large chocolate chip cookie. I consumed it in silence. Other than Brett, and the complications around his death, we didn't have much to talk about. I preferred that. Ever since reading about Brett's death I'd been restless and on the move. I kicked off tennis shoes. Confident we hadn't been followed, my body let go. The full stomach and steady sun made me sleepy. I stretched out on my back, closed my eyes. The mind drifted. It produced images of the small round lake.

Elise said, "It would be great if you let me massage your hand."

My mind no longer drifted.

The blanket made spongy sounds on sand. Elise settled next to me, on her back. "Would it be okay to massage it?"

"Why?"

"With Brett gone, I don't have anyone to take care of. Don't suggest I get a dog. I heard it all day yesterday."

Elise took my bad hand and placed it on her stomach. She kneaded the stumpy appendage. Slowly, warmly, both thumbs found grooves. It was a strange sensation. Her hand movements reminded me of a person knitting.

I said, "Karen's grandfather used to say everything is perfect. We humans just mess things up. Now is perfect."

"I agree."

Elise continued to massage my hand. Sun warmed us in the bowl of white stone. I closed my eyes and saw a blue after-image. The after image morphed into reddish gray. The reddish gray vanished from my thoughts. Tenseness in my hand vanished. I think Elise felt me let go, because she moved my hand to my hip, gently patted it, then rolled away, onto her side.

I fell asleep for half an hour. When I woke up, Elise was reading a book about Mayan civilization. Wind had slipped over the granite and invaded our tranquility. On the walk down, and on the drive to Elise's house, we said little. We did, however, exchange smiles. We'd become good friends without the complications of sex.

Nine

Ever since Whitmer phoned to tell me about someone at Ralston Beach wearing a yellow Blizzard Casino windbreaker, who turned out to be Roberto, the call had bothered me. Why would Whitmer risk exposure by directing me to what he referred to as a regular customer? If Roberto were busted, wouldn't he try to trade Whitmer's name for a lesser sentence? Dealers are more prized than users. Whitmer claimed to be a good friend of Brett's—thus motivation for alerting me about a man in a Blizzards windbreaker—yet he exhibited no emotion when our conversation turned to Brett's murder.

What was the Star Wars addict up to? Did he know that I knew Roberto?

After dinner, I headed to Whitmer's house. His truck was in the driveway. I parked and went to the door. A throbbing glow came from within, though no lights seemed to be on. I heard muffled explosion noises. This visit, moving slower, I saw a doorbell. It sounded with a run of notes reminiscent of a military parade. I knew it was loud enough to be heard over whatever battle was on TV because the sounds inside cut. Behind me and above, the Arts and Crafts lamp popped on brightly.

The door opened. Whitmer looked surprised, but in a pleasant way. "Hey, Bro," he said. "Come on in. I was just eating."

I opened the screen door for myself, entered the living room. The screen door hushed closed on its own.

Behind me, Whitmer shut the door. "Hungry?"

"I rarely turn down free food."

It was like a replay of the other time I'd been there. Vegetarian pizza on the redwood burl coffee table, shiny can of Diet Coke, TV remote controller, lighted phone, the big-screen television atop a table in the dining area. Whitmer went to the kitchen. He wore fuzzy pointed elf slippers. I looked at the Star Wars figurines, then to the TV. Storm Troopers in white garb were in a freeze-frame, unable to resume battle until a button was pushed.

Whitmer returned with a plate, a few napkins and a Diet Coke. I took a slice of pizza and sat in the same chair as before, balancing the plate on my thighs. I said thanks and took a bite of pizza. Whitmer glanced at his phone.

I said, "Tell me about your relationship with Roberto Ramirez."

"Who?" No facial reaction, though Whitmer looked down rather than at me.

"You know who."

"Easy, bro. Stress is bad for your health."

While working for Sherman Investigations, I usually got better results by being firm yet not pushy.

"I'm just curious. What is it with you and Roberto?"

Whitmer set down his pizza slice. He licked two fingers. "We have what I guess you'd call a symbiotic relationship."

"One in which you rat him out to a stranger?"

"Hey. You're no stranger. You're Brett's bro. I checked you online. What you said about being B-ball friends turned out to be true. You and I want the same thing. Find who killed Brett."

"You probably do want that. But bad enough to put yourself in potential legal jeopardy? If I sent the police after Roberto, why wouldn't he name you? Last time I was here, you invited me to put cards on the table. Now it's your turn."

Whitmer looked to the Star Wars posters behind and above me. He seemed to search them for inspiration. Whitmer scratched one pole of a dark sideburn, then the other. "The thing is," he said, "life's a movie. We're just playing our roles. Don't take it so seriously."

"What happens after the screen goes blank?"

"Nobody knows. It's the big finale. People think they know, but till it happens it's all guesses. I just go along for the ride."

"But you make choices. Like sending me to find Roberto at Ralston Beach. After basically telling me you sold him drugs."

Whitmer picked up a pizza slice. He took a bite. He pointed to mine. "Choose to enjoy. Eat up. You want to find Brett's killer. I get it."

"Now you're saying you don't really care much about it?"

"I'm saying I'm along for the ride. I don't get stressed. Just a second."

Whitmer went to the kitchen. He returned carrying a can of Diet Coke. He set the shiny can next to me on a side table, removed a Stars Wars creature figurine, which he petted at depositing it on the dining table. Whitmer then sat in front of his row of pizza, remote controller and phone silently playing a cartoon.

I said, "I kind of get what you're saying. Now to curious question number two: How did Elise react to the symbiotic relationship you had with Brett?"

"Far as I know, she didn't. Every transaction was when she was away. Then last year, she moved out."

"Where do you get your stuff?"

"You're asking too many questions. Questions you don't want the answers to." Whitmer picked up a pizza slice. He grinned tautly while chewing. The grin became tighter as he swallowed.

"You might keep in mind that what you know could come back to hurt you."

"Is that a threat?"

"If you quit asking questions, no."

I sensed a fissure in his life-is-just-a-movie routine. I cranked the dial higher. "Why does it bother you if I ask questions? Did Brett know where you get your stuff? Would that have put him in danger?"

Whitmer scratched his lower lip with his upper teeth. He pointed the remote toward the big-screen TV. "Hey, you want to watch a movie?"

Experience told me I'd learn nothing more from Whitmer that night. Rather than become insistent, and drive him off, I said I had to get back to prepping for the state boards.

Whitmer said, "Cool."

The battle on TV recommenced before I was out the door.

I'd just turned onto Cathedral Road when Antonio called. "He's here. Drinking in the bar. He asked Mike if he'd seen a guy with a hand like yours." Mike Conlon, bartender at Antonio's. "Says he owes the man fifty dollars. Don't worry, Mike knows to never talk about a customer."

"Waiters?"

"The same."

"I'm coming in."

"No trouble in my restaurant."

"Not from me," I said, and hung up without giving Antonio a chance to discourage me from driving to town.

I took money from my wallet and stuffed it in my left front pocket. I put on the long-sleeved sweatshirt that was always on the backseat. An orange and black San Francisco Giants cap came next. I couldn't think of a path ahead without a conclusion wherein either Mr. Yellow Windbreaker or I prevailed. He was after me. I could either run or advance matters from my end.

At Antonio's, I parked in back, passing the black Range Rover on the way. I walked to the rear of the big SUV, looked around to be sure no one watched, clicked a photo of the license plate, two of the vehicle. My phone went into a pocket. I pulled the baseball cap low and walked into the restaurant.

At seeing Reina, the hostess, I put a finger to my lips. Her eyes opened wide. She didn't move as I passed the menu-covered lectern she presided over. I entered the bar. Mike Conlon busied himself drying glasses. No one was next to the man I was there to see; he exuded a twitchy hostility. I sat to his right, keeping an open stool between us. My bad hand stayed in the kangaroo pouch of my sweatshirt. I ordered a bottle of Sierra Nevada Pale Ale. A baseball game played on the elevated TV.

I spoke in a countrified California twang. "No need for a glass."

Conlon said, "Got it," and acted as if he'd never seen me.

I paid with a ten and left the change on the wood counter. I took a swallow, glanced leftward. The man was swacked. He blinked so hard his whole right eye squished down. His right hand jiggled on the counter. His feet wriggled on the floor. He looked my way. He closed that right eye, as if to focus with his left.

I said, "What brings you to Tahoe?"

Well-built, his shoulders were broad. Even in low bar light the scar running across the top of his right eyebrow stood out.

He said, "What brings you?"

"Mud flaps. I'm here because of mud flaps."

The man labored to think straight. "What the fuck're you talking about?"

"I sell mud flaps. Got Northern California, Oregon and Washington. I get paid to see some of the best country in America."

His dark eyes jumped about. That wouldn't come from alcohol. "Sounds boring."

"I never tire of it. I'm my own boss, free as a bird at the company's expense. What do you do?"

"I mind my own business." He looked me over. His red-hued face betrayed tension. "Do I know you from somewhere?"

"Not unless you've spent time in Grants Pass. Oregon. That's where I'm from."

It was only a matter of time—possibly a short time—and he'd notice my right hand stayed in the sweatshirt's front pocket. And he was on the hunt for a mangled right hand. I finished my beer and left the bar. I went to my car. I drove to the side of the building. This gave view of the restaurant entrance and the Range Rover.

He came out weaving. Crossing paths with a couple, he stared at them, turned and watched them go into Antonio's. He tripped at getting into the Range Rover, backed around and exited the lot. I waited till he couldn't see me pull out and followed south on the highway.

He traveled the same route as the other time I followed the Range Rover. He turned left toward Luther Pass. A car followed my left turn. I drove onto the road's dirt shoulder and let it pass. The three vehicles climbed, then headed down. The Range Rover reached Carson Valley. It pulled off at the river, near the stop sign where the road met Highway 88. I found a spot with room to park safely, turned off the headlights and looked down upon the valley.

The car ahead of me reached the stop sign, turned left. The driver's door of the Range Rover popped open. Mr. Yellow Windbreaker got out—sans windbreaker—wobbled a few steps. I took my binoculars from their case. I went outside, leaned across the Subaru's hood and focused the binoculars. The wind was light, the evening not cold for the area at that hour. It struck me that I was alive and loving every minute of it.

A car passed; its lights swept over me. It didn't slow.

The man wandered on the asphalt. His head went up and down, apparently having a conversation with someone imagined or with himself. He shook his right fist as though making a threat. He tripped and caught himself on the front of his vehicle. He shook his head hard, like he was trying to rid it of something unwanted. The car that had passed me reached the stop sign. Mr. Yellow Windbreaker ambled in its direction, shaking that right fist. The car peeled out to the left. The sizzle of its burning tires carried all the way up to me.

It took effort, but the man made it to the Range Rover, and inside. He sat for five minutes. I couldn't see if he was still having an imaginary conversation. The SUV's lights came on. It chugged ahead. I thought of how nice it would be if Mr. Yellow Windbreaker drove off the mountain highway, preferably where the roadside fell away steeply.

The Range Rover headed up the valley. It wove much as its driver had when walking outside at Antonio's. I stayed far behind it, over Carson Pass, careful not to reveal myself this time. Heading down I hoped he might lose control on a turn. The hour was moonless. The only illumination a driver had was a vehicle's headlights. Soon after Caples Lake, I caught those lights turning left onto the road to Kirkwood Ski Resort.

Anyone coming in behind, in the dark, pre-ski season and few people living at Kirkwood, would arouse suspicion in a guilty man. I chose to end the night with two gains: the license plate number of the person I believed killed Brett, and knowledge of where he lived or was staying.

*　　*　　*

After making inquiries based on our seven a.m. conversation, Clint Sherman called. His voice grew froggier and dryer with each passing year. Clint said, "The vehicle is a rental, from Sid's Cars, Trucks and Vans, in Burbank. Nowadays, everybody's afraid they'll get sued. A grand couldn't buy the name of the renter. I got hung up on. I tried an old associate who's now with LAPD. He apologized and said he couldn't help me."

I had information about the suspect, at least my suspect. The scar above the right eyebrow. Plus the license plate number, from which the police would be able to obtain the name of the man who rented the vehicle, assuming he didn't use a fake I.D. I drove to the South Lake Tahoe Police Department and asked to see Sergeant Stevens.

After showing my driver's license and walking through the metal detector, a brief call was made. A deputy marched me down the same hallway as before. The door to the office where Stevens and others worked was open. I knocked on its frame, expecting Stevens to frown and grumble at seeing me.

He looked up from a computer screen. His intent face sprung a cheerful smile matched by rosy cheeks. "I figured next time I saw you would be at another crime scene." A happy camper, Stevens waved me in. "This just came in the mail. From Elise. I've been too slammed to get to it. I think I'll open it now. Let's see what she sent me."

I went to Stevens' desk. He pointed to a small package about two inches thick. He tore off the outer wrapping like a child opening a Christmas present. He plucked out a white box. Stevens removed its lid. Inside, placed on white tissue paper, a silver-plated belt buckle. My heart pounded blood through my head so fast it felt like my head would burst. I swerved around the desk. My eyes stayed on the box.

Stevens' eyes stayed on the box, too. "I guess Elise is thanking me for looking out for her."

His smile widened. I collared Stevens with a slash of my left arm. I rammed my body into his and drove him backwards past a metal filing cabinet and against the wall. His glasses askew, I wrestled Stevens to the floor. I let him make quick work of spinning over me and planting a knee in the center of my back. My goal was to keep him away from that box. He yanked my right arm backwards and up, straining the socket.

Stevens shouted, "What's wrong with you? Jealous? Is that it?"

His knee felt like a sharp object ripping my shoulder blades apart. I gasped at the pain. I got out, "Potassium cyanide."

Stevens shouted, "I'm going to fry your ass for this!"

"Cyanide. In the box."

Neither of us spoke. The only sounds were of harsh breathing. The knee let up some.

"At Brett's," I said, "one of these boxes was open on the dining room table. Same belt buckle."

The knee let up more. Stevens released my right arm. I turned over, rolling him off me. Two officers rushed into the room. They located Stevens and me on the floor. The younger of the two drew a pistol and pointed it toward the floor.

Stevens rose his right hand as if taking an oath. "Stay right there. Stay right where you are."

The two officers, wide eyed, complied.

Stevens picked himself off the ground. He stepped to behind his desk.

I said, "Don't touch it. It'll have cyanide on it."

Stevens looked to the officers. One who looked to be in his fifties, chunky, huffed as much as Stevens and me. The other I gauged to be in his late twenties, with brown eyes that shined. The revolver dangled below his right hip.

He said, "You sure everything's okay?"

Stevens said, "Get Alicia Froug in here. Tell her full PPE. Evidence bags. Face shield over mask." He pointed at me. "For now, on the floor."

The younger officer said, "Yes, sir," slipped his gun into the holster, snapped it and disappeared.

The older policeman said, "What should I do?"

"Return to your duties. Everything's under control." Stevens turned from looking at the white box to looking down at me. "Elise's name and address are typed. Mine, too. What about at Brett's?"

"I didn't see what it came in."

"I remember now. White box, open on the dining table with a bunch of other stuff."

"Obviously new."

Stevens' eyes seemed dilated; he operated on automatic pilot. He backed up to where his body met the wall, and slowly slid to the floor. A few feet to my left, he offered his right hand. We shook.

Stevens said, "I might owe you my life."

Above his head, light poured through a closed window. Dust motes twirled within a glowing, yellowish square. I remembered almost picking up the silver belt buckle at Brett's. I'd been inches from poisoning myself,

Alicia Froug strode into the room. Stout, exuding strength, she took in the scene. Behind her came the young officer with shiny brown eyes. Cloaked in flowing blue reminiscent of Sky Lake, Froug said, "What do you think you've got?"

Stevens said, "Potassium cyanide. Like at Boyd's."

Froug reached into the blue cloth folds off her PPE and extracted a cell phone. She tapped it. She set the phone on the adjacent desk. Froug recited date, time and location. She said, "Sergeant James Stevens, City of South Lake Tahoe PD, will describe objects he contacted me about. He will explain how he came into possession of them, and anything else he deems relevant. From there I'll secure the objects and take them for analysis. Jim?"

Stevens stood. His footing solid, he spoke decisively. Detail followed detail in chronological order. This included me knocking him to the ground and saying, "Potassium cyanide." He did not go back and make corrections. He didn't once clear his throat.

After Stevens made his statement, officer Froug fed her phone a brief description of what she bagged. She shooed Stevens and me from the room. A female officer was posted just outside the door.

Froug said, "No one in or out. I don't care who it is, you block this door. No exceptions." To Stevens, she added, "I'll take air samples, make sure it's clear. You two can go to the break room and get some junk food. I'll have someone let you know when all's clear."

Stevens stopped walking. Froug and I stopped walking.

Stevens said, "Alicia, what do you do for fun?"

"I read up on how people poison each other. You'd be surprised how rich the literature is."

Stevens nodded. "I'm sure I would be."

Froug said, "I've got to get my airborne assess kit." She turned left down a hallway.

Stevens said, "Let's see what there is to eat. I never go there."

The police department's break room consisted of two metal tables lined with metal chairs, two vending machines, an upside down water jug, paper cups in a pull-out stack, and a refrigerator that looked like it was picked up at a flea market. No magazines or newspapers. No pictures on the walls. No one else occupied the dreary room.

Stevens took my order: two packs of two peanut-butter cookies. He went another direction, getting barbecued chips and spicy pork rinds. He tore open both packages. He chomped away. I saw that beneath his stoic exterior his motor still ran hot. He'd come within a second of dying.

I said, "I came to tell you about last night. I sat with the guy from Sky Lake, in the bar at Antonio's. I followed him to Kirkwood. I got his license plate number."

Stevens swallowed a chunk of pork rind. He got it down and went to the water dispenser. "I'm listening."

I went over what happened the night before. I emailed photos of the license plate and the black Range Rover to Stevens' South Lake Tahoe PD email address.

Stevens said, "Since he didn't recognize you, couldn't you be mistaken? Maybe he wasn't the guy who confronted you at Sky Lake."

"The odds of that are the same as the odds of you getting a neatly wrapped belt buckle from Elise that matched the one sent to Brett. Now, I've given you everything I can think of. If I think of anything else, I'll call. For now, I've got to get back to the books."

Ten

My phone sang. *Elise* shone on its face in white letters. Far as I knew, before Brett was killed, he, and the neighbors I met at the strange gathering honoring Brett, were the only locals Elise was in regular contact with. Until Brett quit water skiing, Elise had been on the road as much as she'd been home. Emails with other models and Annabee could carry one only so far. I remembered the years of spending most of my hours alone, after my hand was sliced, until meeting Karen.

I clicked the phone and said hello.

Elise said, "Jim Stevens called. He told me what happened. He says not to open any packages unless it's from someplace I ordered from. He says to throw any ads in the outside garbage, and don't open envelopes unless it's a bill I regularly get."

"It's good advice. I should have thought of it."

"I'm scared. Can I come over?"

"I don't think it's a good idea."

"You can study. I'll bring a book. You won't even know I'm there."

"If the suspect follows you, he'll know where I live."

"You won't see me? At the hour I want a drink?"

"Are you manipulating me, or what?"

"I hope or what. Okay, I'll say it. I'm lonely and afraid I'll get drunk again today. Are you happy now?"

Mr. Yellow Windbreaker had had an easy line of fire, with no witnesses, and didn't shoot. Should I take solace in that, or should I stay one hundred percent on guard?

"How about this? I won't go to your place, because I think he knows it and it's possible he's keeping watch. How about you drive Pioneer Trail toward Stateline. Go a little too fast. For miles. Keep checking the rear-view mirror for a black Range Rover. If you're one hundred percent sure he's not behind you, come over. As long as you haven't been drinking, come by at four. I'll be studying. Take Cathedral Road till you see my car in a carport on the left, two miles in."

I studied. Then I set about cleaning the house, putting throw pillows back, washing dishes left in the sink, doing everything a man does to prepare for having a woman over for an at home date. I justified my interest in Elise's visit by having a question for her, a question that came to mind driving back to The Lodge the night before. Or was the question I wanted answered really an excuse to receive the attentions of a three-time *Vogue* cover model?

Elise arrived a few minutes early. She carried a bakery bag that she swung aside as she gave me the cheek kisses routine.

Elise extracted a monster chocolate chip cookie, like the one at Cradle Lake, and a thick hardback book by an author whose name I didn't recognize. She set them on the pine dining table for ten. Elise walked to the fireplace, stepped out of sandals so they dropped on the granite hearth. She walked to me and offered a for-the-camera smile. She put out her right hand. I shook it.

Elise said, "Good to see you, Doctor Boy Scout." She spun around and plopped on the long green cloth couch that ran perpendicular to the fireplace. She patted the couch cushion, to her left, inviting me to join her.

I went to the fireplace, kicked off my tennis shoes. Elise rose her arm in an arc, again encouraging me to sit next to her.

I thought of Karen, who was the best thing in my life. I'd never cheated on anyone, not even as a dumb teenager. Was this cheating, or soothing an anguished soul?

I settled in. Elise took my half hand and brought it to her stomach.

She massaged my hand like she had at Cradle Lake.

Elise said, "I need this. It calms me."

I looked across the oversized room, with a high ceiling of oiled knotty pine. "Something tells me you usually get what you need."

"You are so wrong I won't even start."

"It was meant as a compliment."

Elise said, "I'm touchy about my appearance. It makes people think I have it made, when other than putting me at the party where I met Brett, the only good it's done is create income."

"And taken you all over the world. Made you famous."

Elise slowly shook her head. "Screw that." She ceased the massage, took a breath, gazed across the spacious room. "What am I going to do with myself?" As if remembering, Elise resumed rubbing my hand at the missing fingers spot and the stump of a middle finger. "My mind keeps going in circles. It's driving me crazy."

"For now," I said, "how about if we just sit here and enjoy the universe? Don't think, don't talk or anything."

She nodded. Again it struck me how quiet—and exposed—it was there, amidst trees above the dark lake, the nearest human half a mile away.

The front door opened without a knock. Something rolled across the wood floor. "I made it. I'm here!"

Elise and I popped off the couch. The Lodge's entry looked out upon the whole of the great room. My mom let go of the pull line on a gray, wheeled suitcase. She shut the door behind her and came across the room beaming like she'd just won the lottery. I hadn't seen my mom since graduating from Sacramento State. I hadn't seen her since before my hand was ruined. I had not seen my mother, who lived in rural Alaska, in ten years. An anti-tech person, Mom had never gotten a cell phone, and refused to use a computer. Our only communications, about once a year, were letters sent through the post office. The most recent was informing her that Karen and I had moved to South Lake Tahoe, giving Mom our new address and post office box number.

Tired from her journey, her face blotched with fatigue, T-shirt and jeans rumpled, Mom thrust out her right hand. "Karen. I'm happy to finally meet you. Your husband and I don't communicate much, but he's made it clear how happy you make him."

Mom's brown hair hung to shoulder tops. Her eyes swiveled from Elise to me and back. "You two are a damn good fit."

Elise looked like she wanted to be drawn into the fireplace, up and out the chimney.

I was not the cool under pressure guy I'd been on basketball courts. My mouth opened. Nothing came out.

Mom pumped Elise's hand. "Karen, I'm Linda Taylor. It's nice to finally put a face to the name."

Elise said, "Actually, my name is Elise."

Mom's face squinched together in confusion.

I said, "This doesn't look right. It's not what it seems."

"Jeff and I are friends," Elise said.

I looked up. Hanging from the ceiling's apex was a painted red, wood bird chandelier with light bulbs perched on its shoulders, and one in its mouth and one poking out its rear. The most hideous piece of home furnishing I'd ever witnessed, the red wood bird seemed to mock me.

My cheeks stung. "We're just friends."

My mom examined Elise from head to toe. "With friends like this, who needs a wife?"

I'd forgotten about my mom's bawdy laugh. She let it fly.

Elise said, "I should go."

Mom said, "Don't go because of me."

I was back to being devoid of words.

Elise walked to the fireplace, grabbed her sandals, set them on the floor and stepped into them. "Thank you. But I need to go." Elise whispered, "Bye, Boy Scout." Her face scarlet, she picked up her book and exited out the door my mom had just come through. She closed it gently; I saw strain on Elise's face through the glass upper half of the front door.

Mom said, "Where's the real Karen?"

"Back East, visiting family."

"I saw nothing. I'll say nothing."

"Really, Elise and I are just friends."

I sat across from Mom, in one of the wicker chairs. The square pine coffee table was between us. How in the world could I explain Elise and I popping off the couch like we were caught at something?

Mom whistled as she took in the The Lodge. "This is like a mansion. An honest to God mansion."

"Don't be impressed. We're renting."

Mom kept looking up and around. When her chin came down, she saw my hand. Her eyes shut so tightly it was as if she'd been struck in the face.

"Jeffy," she whispered. "Jeffy, I'm a louse for forgetting. Please forgive me."

My mom sobbed. I tried to console her. She looked at my hand, snapped her eyes up and wept louder.

After a time, exhausted from three flights and a trip that began the afternoon of the day before, my mother rolled onto her side. She mumbled something, then slowly coasted into a trembling sleep. I went to the hall, opened a closet and took out a blanket. I spread the blanket over my mom.

She mumbled, "Love you, Jeffy."

It was like nighttime during my childhood, Mom and I alone in that converted barn at the end of a boondocks gravel road. She'd whisper she loved me as she fell asleep on a used checkered couch she bought for twenty bucks. In my earliest memories, I'd slept there with her. When I was about five I made my own abode, in a little dome tent closer to the woodstove. I felt the warmth, love and privacy of my childhood. It lasted a few seconds.

Eleven

I carried my mother's big gray suitcase upstairs. The second floor, above three downstairs bedrooms, was a long dormitory-style room with six iron-frame beds, a bathroom and a separate shower. I took towels from a wood cabinet and stocked the bathroom. I went downstairs and studied till Mom woke up at shortly before seven o'clock.

I lit a fire. The middle of September, the house in the full shade of tall evergreens all day, evenings were already cold.

Things settled down. It was as if Mom were embarrassed at showing up unannounced, and perhaps by her sobbing. Maybe she was mostly tired. Her hazel eyes lacked sharpness. Horizontal lines crossed her forehead like unmarked sheet music. Her hair dyed its light brown, the passage of time also showed in a general thickening of her frame. She'd always been wiry, not thin like Karen but a strong, feisty wiry. None of the changes were extreme. They were manifestations of the decade that had passed without seeing each other.

I heated pumpkin soup and toasted slices of French bread dusted with Parmesan cheese. The food brought light to Mom's face. We sat across from each other at the long dining table. Mom couldn't help herself: she took glances at my hand.

I said, "Where's Del?"

Mom dipped a chunk of bread in her soup. She bit off its crispy tip. Her eyes stayed on the bowl. "We're taking a break."

"A permanent one?" If Mom and Del had broken up, it would explain the surprise visit.

"Not that. I just couldn't look at him, day after day, the two of us stuck inside. He… Del's gone too far. I don't want to endure it every day."

"His drinking's that out of control?"

Mom looked up from her bowl of soup. "He took Social Security at sixty-two. Since he retired, he's come down with religion."

I pictured Del's stringy gray hair, a beer belly nurtured by daily twelve packs, bowlegged posture from his cowboy life before coming to California at forty. He moved slow, he talked slow. He was one hell of a nice guy.

"What kind of religion?"

"AA. He's got it bad."

"Isn't that good?"

Mom shook her hair, blew at strands dangling close to her eyes. She took another chomp of crispy bread. "It would be, except he takes it too far. If I have a second glass of wine with dinner, he looks at me like I'm going straight to hell someday. And he keeps branching out. Last week, I come out in the morning and there's Del on the floor. He's back-flat on a yoga mat, eyes closed, breathing in through his nose, then groaning 'aum' breathing out through his mouth. He looked like a beached whale in need of a haircut."

"That's funny."

"Those yoga pants weren't funny. Neither was the empty yoga mat on the carpet next to him. Del opens his eyes, pats the mat. He says, 'Join in, Honey. It's a new dawn.'"

I laughed so hard I bumped the table, spilling our soup. This set mom to laughing. She tipped her forehead onto an open hand, which went up and down with her laughs. Tears that came now were different from the afternoon tears.

She said, "We shouldn't be laughing," and laughed harder.

"But it's funny as hell."

"That man," Mom said. "That Delvin Andrew Beveridge."

We ate. She asked questions about the house, what Karen was up to, and if I had a job lined up. We shared the big chocolate chip cookie.

Mom said, "I've been cooped up for a day and a half. I'm going for a walk. Safe to walk here at night?"

"The bears are mostly harmless. I'll go with you. Let me feed the fire first."

We headed out carrying flashlights. We passed Mom's rental sedan, parked parallel to the road, and walked along pavement toward the highway. It was curvy yet flat in that direction. Wind rustled through the forest.

Mom said, "That woman today?"

"Yeah?"

"She looks like a fashion model. I mean like you see in magazines."

"She is."

"Hey. My son's committing adultery with a genuine fashion model."

"I'm not."

Mom poked me with an elbow. "I kind of hope you are. I never did anything crazy. Except maybe hopping on that plane yesterday on a whim."

"Does Del know where you went?"

"Hell yes. Just needed a break."

We walked until the cold got to me. After her years in Alaska, my mom seemed impervious to cold. Arriving back at the house, a raccoon was giving the wired-shut garbage can a battle. Mom ran straight at the creature. She didn't try to scare it off with a flashlight, like I had. She raced right up to it and shouted, "You *get*. I'll kick you, you little bastard!"

The raccoon scurried between pine trees into blackness. It's never too late to learn from your mother.

Morning. I explained to Mom my need to study. This was true, as was the fact I didn't know how to spend a day with my own mother. I busied myself making tea, pancakes, and pointless conversation. How could it be that after eighteen years of just the two of us living together, Mom raising me alone, I had little to say to her?

Guilt, self reproach, and knowing I wasn't stepping up to the moment surged through me. Still, my thoughts veered to Brett Boyd's demise, which I decided to delay telling Mom about. She needed time to settle in some more before receiving the news.

Mom said, "I think I'll drive a three-sixty around Lake Tahoe. Stop for lunch on the way. Give you time to study. That okay with you?"

I said it was okay with me, and hoped my relief didn't show. At her leaving, I recorded Mom's first cell phone number. She'd purchased the phone on a stopover of her trip. I entered my cell number into her phone, showed her how to retrieve it and walked with her out the front door.

Mom whispered, "Bye, Boy Scout."

She laughed all the way to her car.

I commenced preparing for the state boards. That lasted twenty minutes before I searched the internet for silver coated belt buckles with "Think Out Of The…" etched into them. I found only three references to them, accompanied by photos, posted on fake-name

Twitter accounts. It was as if they were part of a secret circle.

Jim Stevens called.

I said, "To what do I owe this honor? Wait, first tell me the lab results."

"Probably would have killed me. I'm going to catch the sicko."

"Any fingerprints on the package?"

"Negative. This guy's thorough."

"And crazy."

Stevens said, "What are you doing this morning?"

"What do you think I'm doing? I'm searching online for those belt buckles."

"If you want to meet the man who sells them, be at the department in half an hour."

I left a note on the dining table, just in case my mom returned before I did, saying I'd be gone until sometime in the afternoon.

As soon as Stevens saw me at his office doorway, he picked up his patrolman's cap, told the woman officer to his right he'd be gone until early afternoon, added the chief knew this and walked briskly to the same patrol car we'd taken to Sky Lake. No hello. No handshake. Not hostile. All business.

I asked where we were headed.

"Rancho Cordova."

That's the first city east of sprawling Sacramento on Highway 50. We traversed the granite of Echo Summit, dropped thirty miles along the zig-zagging American River. Falling in elevation to grasslands, we entered the vast Sacramento Valley. Stevens kept his eyes on the road and didn't speak. I matched him.

He cracked first. Stevens touched his glasses, lifted his chin. "How long since you've seen Elise?"

"Yesterday."

To both sides yellow grass, dry as straw, covered the ground until reaching buildings. The river had disappeared long before, angling away from the highway.

Stevens' face tightened. "So that's why she didn't answer the phone."

We barreled toward Rancho Cordova.

I said, "I think you'll do better at finding Brett's killer if we don't talk about Elise."

"I'll find the killer."

We left the freeway, and proceeded slowly on cracked asphalt. We weren't in Rancho Cordova proper but in a stretch of land between suburbia and open countryside. We passed a gravel mining operation. We bounced on until reaching cyclone fencing as tall as that of a state prison. Inside were rows of big rigs, with open spaces where many had departed for the day, and a warehouse as enormous as an airport hanger. Painted in burgundy on the sides of the big rigs: DAVIS ENTERPRISES — WE HAUL ALL. Stevens drove past the warehouse to an office. It was fifteen degrees warmer in the Sacramento Valley than up at Tahoe.

I followed Stevens inside. A young woman about my age, wearing jeans and a gray T-shirt with the name of a school printed across its front, sat at a desk with two computers in front of her and a mound of paper between them.

Stevens removed his cap. "Jim Stevens to see Mr. Davis. He's expecting me."

"Everyone calls him Pat." The woman pointed to a door behind her. "Go on back. No need to knock."

Stevens marched ahead. I kept my right hand in a pocket.

Pat Davis rose from behind a scarred wood desk that looked older than him, which I guessed was fifty-something years. Fleshy, with ruddy cheeks, he waved toward two brown leather chairs. He lowered himself onto a third one. It creaked like a saddle. Davis fiddled with a cowboy string tie that had a turquoise stone where in a regular tie would be its cloth knot. The room's wood paneling had aged into the color of baked ham.

Stevens and I recited our names.

Davis smiled. A chip in one of his upper front teeth somehow added to the informal atmosphere of the place. Davis said, "My dad started those belt buckles as a hobby when he retired. Over time, they developed a following. He had to hire a couple when he couldn't do 'em justice anymore. I purchase the raw materials. They forge them in their garage. We never reveal the location. We never advertise. It creates a mystique. Now that I've bored you, how in the world do you connect them silver belt buckles to a murder and an attempted one?"

Stevens explained matters to Davis in the same methodical way he did everything.

Davis wiped his lips. "I don't like it, but I hear you."

Stevens said, "It's a guess, but a reasonable one, that whoever's spraying cyanide on your belt buckles may have purchased several at once. If you could give me the names of any bulk purchasers, it would be appreciated."

Pat Davis squeezed a thumb and finger down his ample cheeks. "I would like to accommodate you. God knows we don't want our collectors' items associated with crimes. I called our lawyer. He says since you're not from Sacramento County, you have no legal authority here. Since we're outside city limits, your request should be directed to the county sheriff's office."

Stevens said, "That's why I cleared our informal talk with Sheriff Hatfield. You're welcome to call him about it."

"I have no reason not to believe you. Our lawyer also says we can't hand over any names unless there's a search warrant. We could get in legal trouble for giving out private information."

"The sheriff says he should have a warrant sometime tomorrow, considering there's a murder involved, and the possibility others may follow." Stevens was proving to be sharper than I'd thought.

Davis was a genial man. I guessed his father had been a genial man, sitting behind the same desk in the same beat-up leather chair as his son now did.

Davis said, "If you knew you'd need a warrant, why the rush visit?"

"To ask you to begin a search for either a large purchase, or multiple purchases, by the same buyer. That way the county won't have to sniff through your books. You can have anything you come up with ready. Time counts. You could save somebody's life."

Davis thought this over. "What about Mr. Taylor? Does he ever say anything more than his name?"

Stevens said, "Dr. Taylor is here in an advisory capacity."

"As you can see," I said, "the sergeant needs lots of advice. He rarely knows how to proceed without me advising him."

Davis's laugh boomed off the ham-colored wood paneling. His jowls quaked. His cracked front tooth seemed to poke forth its own delight.

Pat Davis said, "Okay. I'll have Midge, out front, search invoices. If anything's unusual in terms of purchases in the last year, I'll have it ready for Hatfield when he waltzes in with a warrant."

Stevens stood. He gave Davis one of his mini nods. "Thank you."

We headed out. Stevens said to office manager Midge, "South Lake Tahoe PD thanks you for your cooperation."

Stevens replaced his patrolman's cap. I told Midge it was nice to meet her and followed Stevens outside to the white patrol car.

The first day of autumn, sunlight spread like honey over the dry grasslands. I decided to skip a staying silent contest. "Why did you ask me to come today?"

Stevens kept his gaze—really more a stare—on the pavement we rolled over at seventy miles per hour. "For your advice. Without it I'd have no idea how to proceed."

I thought I caught the slightest possible upturn of his mouth, a grin even tinier than his nods.

"You're not pissed at my crack?"

"It helped loosen him up. Not that he was resisting." Whatever facial expression had eked out of Stevens disappeared. "Besides, I owe you one."

"I don't think you operate that way."

For the first time with me in that patrol car, both the Sky Lake and Rancho Cordova trips, Stevens looked over at me. His eyes went back to the road. "I figured you'd figure out where the belt buckles come from. I didn't want you to come down here freelancing on your own."

Again Stevens proved himself sharper than I'd have thought. And he became downright chatty.

Stevens said, "Roberto Ramirez emailed me four screen shots of the person of interest. I sent 'em statewide. Nothing yet. But with the license plate of the Range Rover, which is a rental, and the photos, we'll get him. The only problem is time. We don't want another incident."

"Definitely."

"Why didn't you tell Antonio to have the bartender secure the man's glass with a cloth napkin, by its base? We could've tried for fingerprints. The mug might've been too wet, but we could've tried."

"Didn't think of it. I just rushed to the restaurant at getting a call. The last time he stayed less than ten minutes. Didn't want to miss a chance to talk to him."

"No matter. We'll get him."

I said, "Regarding the license plate, since it's a rental he could already be driving something else. He probably used a fake I.D. to rent it. You know?"

Stevens shook his head no farther left and right than his nods went up and down. Then he went wild and lifted his right hand from the steering wheel. He trained his forefinger on me. "Don't start freelancing again."

My phone pinged its chirpy tune. I rose from the seat, slipped the phone out of a rear pocket of jeans, checked the name. I slid the phone back in place.

Stevens said, "Elise?"

"My mom."

"Yeah, right. You were awfully quick putting it away."

I got the phone out and cut into voice mail. "Hi. Where are you?"

I turned the phone toward Stevens. "Just passed a place called Meeks Bay. Where's the best hike between here and your place? I want to get out and stretch the legs."

I described the long C-curve above Emerald Bay. I suggested Mom park in the lot there and walk up Eagle Creek to Eagle Lake. "Half an hour at most."

We said goodbyes. I returned my phone to a back pocket. Stevens didn't say another word all the way to South Lake Tahoe.

Twelve

I was studying when my mom came in through the front door.

"What a hike! Beautiful. Emerald Bay, with that island in the middle? The whole thing is great."

Mom's face had good color from sun and excitement. Compared to the day before, she seemed youthful. Her steps were bouncy, her mood ebullient.

Mom said, "Just look at you. I'm so glad I came."

I stood, and indicated she should sit on the green couch. "I need to tell you something. I didn't want to yesterday, right after you arrived."

Mom was too upbeat to catch my tone. "Am I going to be a grandmother?"

"Please, have a seat."

"I hope it's not something with that model."

"Please sit. Take a breath. I have bad news."

Mom's face screwed tight, as it had the day before when she saw my impaired hand for the first time. I told her about reading of Brett's death on my laptop, that he'd been murdered and the police hadn't yet found the killer.

Mom sobbed quietly. She opened her arms. Her sobs increased and for the first time since she came, I hugged my mother. We held each other. For half a minute we were those two people, mother and child, who'd lived alone in the woods. We'd been too close then. Now we weren't close at all. Yet that early bond broke through everything.

The sobbing ebbed. Mom sniffed. She wiped her nose with the sleeve of her sweatshirt. "Brett was the best kid ever. He was the leader, but you weren't far behind. You beat all those city teams." Mom sniffed and wiped her nose again. "I wish I'd gone to more games."

"You watched during the regular season. The others were far away."

"I could've driven to a few more. I couldn't afford the weekend hotels, but I could've driven to Sacramento. Or Fresno. I could've stayed with people I grew up with. I worried about running into my parents. I didn't want any scenes."

Mom went to the kitchen, found paper napkins. She blew her nose.

She sat at the dining table. "Who," Mom said. She blew her nose again. This time when speaking, Mom looked at me. "Who in the world would want to kill Brett?"

"I think I know. Don't know his name, or much about him. But I'm going to find him. I'm going to find him, beat the shit out of him and turn him in."

Mom's eyes dropped again. Her breaths droned heavily. "Do it," she said. "Do it for both of us."

Mom rose. She went to the kitchen. She opened cupboards. "Do you have anything to drink in this big house?"

"Red wine. A few beers. Which do you want?"

Mom smoothed back her hair. Her face grew resolute. "Get out your best wine. We're going to drink a toast to Brett Boyd. Of all you kids on those all-star teams, Brett was the one who was supposed to go all the way."

"For about ten years, he did."

"We'll drink to that, too."

I located the bottle of pinot noir I'd bought for Karen and me to share after learning I'd passed the state boards.

Mom said, "How are you dealing with it? I know you and Brett drifted apart. That happens in your twenties. I also know you stuff your feelings down, keeping the worst from hurting you. But they're still in there."

"When Karen comes back, I'll be fine."

Mom got up and walked around the The Lodge's great room. She patted the top of her head with both hands. "Now I know what the big knife is about."

I called Elise and said we had to have a serious talk. She didn't ask what the talk would be about. Plainly, Elise was starved for company.

I said, "You know the area. Where's a good place to talk privately? But out in the open, in case one of us is followed."

"Are you familiar with Taylor Creek?"

"With that name, how could I not be?"

"Meet me by the ranger station, at the end of the parking lot."

I took Karen's dusky orange Volvo. Since the suspect had seen my Subaru, it would be wise to drive another car. Five o'clock when I arrived, the sun dropped behind the summit of Mt. Tallac. Dark clouds fanned over it in mottled bunches. Afternoon wind whined against birch trees. Their leaves, turning autumnal colors, flashed like gold coins.

Elise pulled up next to the Volvo. She showed surprise at me being in a different car. She got out swinging her flag of blonde hair over a pinkish down jacket. I glanced back toward the highway, to see if she was followed. Two sedans entered the lot in succession. Then a pickup truck. I had no guess at whether Elise had been followed. Being parked in front of the ranger station helped ease my worries.

I locked the car, and signaled for Elise to do the same with hers.

She locked the Mercedes and stepped in my direction. "The kokanee started spawning," she said. "It's amazing."

We headed down a dirt path, crossed a short bridge spanning a dribbling creek and walked through grasslands sprinkled with birch trees. A few minutes later the trail curled over a sandy mound, giving us a view of Taylor Creek. It widened there to fifty or sixty feet. Its water shimmered with phosphorescent vermillion stripes. Kokanee salmon swarmed, their jaws jutting and curved, raging in the last throes of life.

Elise took my arm. "Aren't they incredible?"

They were.

Past where the stream fed the lake, Tahoe's cobalt-blue water seemed an immense sweep of nature's perfection. Beyond it, north, Nevada's Mt. Rose popped into the sky. Much closer, the granite walls above Emerald Bay shone like porcelain. Somehow, I had to work our conversation around to if Elise had an enemy angry enough to poison Brett and burn down the chalet and garage. Trying to bump off Stevens I chalked up to Stevens being lead investigator.

Elise tipped her head onto my shoulder. "Brett and I come every year. We'd come like now, in the beginning, and at the end."

The wind lifted birch branches; leaves skittered across the sandy creek bank. Something instinctive caused me to turn around. A man, forties, clicked a photograph. He smiled easily. He wore a dark sports jacket, white shirt, dark slacks and black shoes. Shaggy brown hair billowed over his ears, obscuring them. Twenty feet away, he raised the camera.

I darted forward. "What are you're doing?"

Again the easy smile. "Chris Crawford, *Tahoe Daily Tribune*. I came to shoot the salmon. You two look so cozy, I couldn't resist. Can I have your names for a caption?"

"Can I see your press I.D.?"

His mouth formed an exaggerated O. He patted back pockets. "I guess I left it at the office." He waved his left hand. His right held the camera. I thought I saw him click it. "I hate sitting on my wallet half the day. So I put it aside. I guess I forgot to grab it on my way out."

I stepped toward him. It wouldn't take much to make him talk.

Elise said, "He just took a picture. I'm used to it."

The man flashed his left palm. "I'm sorry if this offends you. We won't use it. You have my word."

At that the man spun on his shiny hard shoes and crunched his way over sand back to the path. I stepped after him. Elise grabbed my arm.

"The last thing I want is more publicity."

"He's not from a newspaper. He would've had I.D. He didn't take any pictures of the fish."

"We don't know that."

Elise took my good hand, turned me around and towed me. "There's a bench up here. C'mon. It's like three feet above the fish."

I looked back. The man moved quickly. I tried to see if he carried a wallet. His back pockets were covered by the dark jacket.

Elise stopped walking. "Look. Above Mt. Tallac. There's a wall of rain coming over it. It's like the biggest waterfall in the world."

Half a dozen miles away, a dark sheet of water pounded the mountain's stone chest. Thunder rumbled.

The bench was placed at a sharp skinny turn in the stream,

squeezing the water into a howling rush. Vermillion salmon writhed just below our feet. Clouds sailed overhead, blocking light. The air grew charged. The air felt alive.

Elise said, "Is there something you're having trouble saying? You keep getting this look on your face, like you want to say something."

"I'm holding back because I don't want to upset you. You've gone through enough."

"Don't treat me like that. Don't baby me."

"If I or the police are going to find who sent Brett the cyanide, it's important to know if you have enemies. I don't mean someone you argue with, or have a modeling feud with. I mean someone who has an axe to grind huge enough to kill Brett over it."

Elise stood from the bench so quickly I lurched to catch her shoulders; otherwise, she might have fallen into Taylor Creek.

She shook her head. "I don't get it. I don't think I know anybody like that. Wouldn't he go after me instead?"

"What would hurt you more, a quick death, or ending Brett's life, knowing it would haunt you forever? If there is someone who wants to hurt you, he gets more mileage out of ending Brett's life, making you suffer. Maybe he goes after you later? I'm just speculating, but I want to cover every possibility."

I tried to pull Elise back to the safety of the bench. She tore away and staggered upstream. She sagged against a birch tree.

"Are you saying all this could be because of me?"

"I'm just trying to cover the bases."

"I feel like I'm going to puke."

I did not approach Elise. "Didn't Stevens ask you about this possibility?"

"He tries to make it seem like everything's okay. Sometimes he swings by the house. He really is a nice man. He helped Brett through many a night when I was away."

I watched frantic salmon. The sky further darkened.

"This guy isn't likely to stop with Brett and Stevens. Going after Stevens tells me he's like these salmon. He's going to push himself until he dies."

Elise looked at me as if pleading. "How can you be so sure?"

"Do you know how these salmon know which stream to return to?"

"I don't."

"Sense of smell. They cruise this enormous lake for three or four years, then *smell* where to return to the same stream they were born in. They spawn and fertilize eggs to reproduce. Then they die. I smell a death wish with this guy. Trying to kill a cop? That's begging for it."

Elise said, "I hope you're not just trying to scare me, because I'm already hella scared. I hear things at night that aren't there."

Rain pounded us. I looked up but had to look away. The rain was that severe. We ran. By the time we reached the parking lot, the sleeves of Elise's down jacket, flooded, had withered. Our clothes looked like we'd been in one of those dunking booths you see at school carnivals.

I unlocked the doors of the Volvo and motioned for Elise to enter via the passenger door. I hustled around and hopped in.

Elise smoothed her clothes, patted her hair. "I must look a mess."

I turned on the heater. We busied ourselves straightening our clothes. Rain beat the car's metal hood like drumsticks.

Elise took my bad hand with both of hers. "Everybody else only sees Brett of the last couple years. The drinking, the dope. All the craziness. Nobody says it, but I can tell people think I'm relieved it's over. I'm not. I miss him."

I took my hand from hers. "I understand." The pulsating rain filled the Volvo with echoes.

Elise said, "You see the Brett of our early years. You see him like he is in those DVDs. I should give them to you."

Elise looked out at the trees and rain. I assumed she didn't want me to see her cry.

I hadn't watched myself play since my hand was ruined. I'd thrown away all DVDs, newspaper articles and photos of my playing days years before. Would I watch the old me now? I didn't know. It took another minute for the windshield to clear. I thought about how Brett, Wild Man Boyd, had kept DVDs of him playing high school basketball during his years of water skiing fame. They'd been that important to him.

I said, "I should get back to my mom."

Elise looked around the clean inside of the car. "When does Karen come back?"

"Thursday."

Elise said, "Your mom was a hoot the other day."

"She sure was."

Elise leaned back into the seat. She closed her eyes, and wiped them. She sat up tall. "I want to give a dinner party for your mom and Karen. To say thanks for borrowing you during this strange time."

"No promises. Let's see how it goes."

I told Elise I'd follow her home. She promised to flick the porch lights when safely inside.

After that, I went to the beginning of her court, turned around. My back was to anyone who came down the road. Ahead, under rain, the light waning, Elise's house was a substantial dark shadow surrounded by black tree trunks. I wondered about the smiling man with a camera. I tried to recall what he looked like. Anything to remember? An oddity to his speaking voice? Ring or watch? Other than brown hair flopping over his ears, nothing came to mind.

I called my mom and said I guessed I'd be back in an hour. She didn't ask where I was. She likely thought I was with Elise and in a way, that was correct. Darkness fell upon the neighborhood.

The rain slackened. I called Stevens. "Word is you know everyone in the area. Do you know a Chris Crawford? He says he works for the *Daily Tribune*."

"Never heard of him."

I told Stevens about watching kokanee salmon in Taylor Creek with Elise. I began to describe the man who crept up behind us, took our picture and claimed to be a photographer for the *Tahoe Daily Tribune*.

Stevens cut me off. "Call me if this fellow does something more than take a picture."

"Doesn't it strike you as odd, him taking pictures without asking? Claiming he left his wallet at work?"

"Look. I'm a few car thefts and domestic violence reports behind. You just happening to let me know you and Elise were together this afternoon, now that strikes me as odd. Don't call again unless somebody breaks the law."

"But what if—"

Stevens hung up. I looked down the street to Elise's house. The car's heater blasted. I wondered what my mom was going to say at me coming home in damp clothes.

About fifteen minutes later, headlights swung into Elise's court. I ducked as a police cruiser passed the Volvo, a car the driver wouldn't recognize. The police car turned in at Elise's driveway. Headlights blinked off. The cruiser's side spotlight flashed on and swept the area, then went off. The driver's door opened. Out stepped Stevens. He went to the front door. A porch roof kept him dry. Stevens did not wear a patrolman's cap. He knocked on the door, stepped back. He knocked again.

A porch light came on. Stevens gestured with his right hand, nodded, and entered Elise's house. Satisfied no one lurked about, I started the Volvo and headed for Fallen Leaf Lake.

Did I think Elise and Stevens shared a secret romance?

Not a chance.

Back at The Lodge, I threw my clothes in the dryer and took a warm shower. Dressed, I entered the high ceilinged great room. In the kitchen, Mom stirred steaming soup in a cast iron pot.

Not looking at me, Mom said, "Are you hungry, or have you already eaten?"

She couldn't suppress a grin.

"I'm hungry."

After dinner I lit a blazing fire; I'd caught a chill sitting in wet clothes for as long as I had. Mom made tapioca pudding from a box Karen and I brought from Sacramento. Sweet and sticky, she brought us each a bowl and settled in front of jumping yellow flames. I asked Mom if she wanted to talk about Greg Naugle, the Stockton firefighter I'd met two months before his death, who happened to be my father. Who I'd never met nor heard about the whole time I was growing up. Mom had refused to even give me his name.

Mom said, "I'm not interested. We were two kids. I got pregnant. We went our separate ways."

After my dad died, I wrote to my mom telling her about him seeking me out. About how he helped me run down the man who killed Karen's grandfather, Clyde Whitney. Mom never wrote back on the subject.

I said, "We can't just pretend he didn't exist. That I didn't spend time with him before he died."

Mom swallowed a spoonful of pudding. She wiped her mouth. "For you, he exists. For me, I never saw or heard from him after I left town. I'm not interested in hearing about him. In fact, I won't." Mom got up and walked to the kitchen. "End of discussion."

Thirteen

Sometimes a single sentence, or phrase, sticks in the mind. It could be superficial or profound. Maybe it's the sound of the speaker's voice in combination with the words. Or it's something you can't pin down.

"This is my me time."

Roberto said that when I'd surprised him at Ralston Beach. He didn't say a word about the search for Brett's killer. The more times I heard the sentence in my head, in Roberto's voice, the more I became curious regarding what else Roberto did during his *me* time.

The next day, Mom went to tour historic silver mines in Nevada. The trek was to give me privacy for studying. My day included more than studying. Roberto's address wasn't hard to find.

I was out the door soon after my mom left at eight a.m. I drove to town, went right on Tahoe Boulevard, southwest, until taking another right on Stone Valley Road. Roberto's house was in open flatland. Deciduous trees had lost some of their leaves. I found a court where I looked to the side and back of Roberto's place. It was quite a spread for a mid level casino employee. Zillow listed the lot size as an acre, and the size of the house as three thousand square feet. A boat that struck me as a cabin cruiser, shrink wrapped in pale blue polyethylene for the early high-country winter, sat in a trailer along a concrete apron astride the garage. I brought a book in case someone came along and asked questions. If so, I'd employ a had-a-fight-with-the-wife tale. I'd used this to good effect when working for Sherman Investigations.

Rocky trotted into view. At the passenger door of a white Chevy pickup, the German Shepherd sat ramrod still. Roberto appeared, wearing a dark knit cap and light jacket. He opened the door. The dog hopped in, I assumed onto the floor because Rocky wasn't visible through my binoculars. Roberto reversed a half circle and drove off. I gave him a good lead. We retraced my route, crossed onto Highway 50 in South Lake Tahoe and headed for Stateline, passing stores, restaurants and small motels. Even in that mass of buildings, when the view opened up Lake Tahoe looked spectacular. Roberto took a right turn, away from the lake. The road meandered into countryside. The white pickup turned into Whispering Pines Cemetery. I continued going straight, found a place to park. Pine forest served as a buffer between the road and the lines of pale headstones.

The forest had long ago been cleared to make way for the dead. The place held no life. Grass between headstones was a dried-out weedy gray. I found Roberto with the binoculars. From what I saw, the cemetery was empty except dog and master.

I took photographs. I zoomed in on the front of the pickup and captured its license plate.

Roberto stopped. I froze, thinking he may have sensed being watched. Rocky halted, sat at attention. Roberto reached into a pocket, delivered a treat, rubbed the dog behind the ears, then ambled on. I lowered the field glasses and surveyed the view.

Why walk there? Roberto had a more engaging walk from his front door than at that scruffy cemetery.

Coming from behind a brick mausoleum, a workman pushed a wheelbarrow. I put the binoculars to my eyes. A canvas tarp, folded in half, covered a lump in the wheelbarrow's bed. The man wore dirty gloves, a dirty sweatshirt and dirty faded jeans. On his head: a black and silver Raiders football-baseball cap. The cap was pulled low. I took a photograph of the man's face but didn't know how clear it would come out.

The man set the wheelbarrow to pavement next to the bed of the white Chevy pickup. He slipped a navy blue duffel bag from under the folded tarp and deposited it in the truck's bed. A second duffel bag. A third came under the tarp that blanketed the duffel bags. The man nonchalantly wheeled the wheelbarrow into the graveyard, left it and walked to behind the mausoleum. I clicked pictures.

Roberto came into view. He let Rocky off his leash. The dog trotted ahead, halted and waited at the passenger door. Roberto let the German Shepherd in. Roberto hit a lever and swung the passenger seat forward. One-two-three, the duffel bags were secured in the pickup's cab while I took pictures.

Roberto lifted the tarp, folded it over an arm and walked to the deserted wheelbarrow. He deposited the tarp, and then drove off. Who would suspect anything disreputable from this neatly dressed, clean-shaven man taking his dog for its morning walk?

I stayed in the trees. Roberto passed my Subaru. He didn't glance at it. The white pickup disappeared in tree shadows and a long bend in the road. I followed to Blizzard Casino, parked in the lot of a motel on the other side of the highway. The railroad gate at the parking lot's entrance rose. Now hatless, Roberto walked Rocky to the entry kiosk. He exchanged words with a man there, who wore a bright yellow windbreaker, and handed him Rocky's leash. Rocky dutifully went inside the kiosk. Roberto walked to the casino entrance. I looked at my phone. 9:57. Roberto had his routine down to the minute.

Enjoy it while you can, I thought, as Roberto disappeared inside the casino. I wasn't going to introduce any distractions from catching Brett's murderer until after he was nailed. After that I'd bring Billy Whitmer and Roberto to the attention of the police. Their actions hurt Brett. Mine would hurt them, thus fulfilling my tribal duty.

I'd learned—or thought I had—why Whitmer let me know about his dealing with Roberto at Ralston Beach: he wanted me to report Roberto to the police. My guess was Whitmer had it in mind to take over the more lucrative role as supplier rather than remain a small-time dealer. Perhaps he had it in mind to play the role of commander in the movie that played in his head. Maybe stitch military stripes on his fuzzy elf slippers.

Fourteen

On Thursday, attempts to study failed. I paced The Lodge's great room. When bored with that I drove to the Lake Tahoe Airport and paced its modest mall of eating spots and gift shops. My eyes kept watch on the board announcing arrivals.

Karen's flight landed. Passengers descended on portable stairs that rolled up to the jet like you see in old movies. Travelers descended and walked toward glass doors. Most people toted carry-on bags.

Karen emerged from a knot of folks. She didn't rise and dip when walking; she glided. I knew her pulse did not quicken. Karen faced most everything in life with an equanimity I admired, envied, and relied on. Chestnut hair rode blade-like shoulders contained in its familiar ponytail. She saw me. Her beloved smile. I went to Karen and hugged her greedily.

"Taylor. How are you this fine day?"

Karen's voice had what I thought of as an East Coast accent. I lifted her and swung her in a full circle. Her feet sailed behind her horizontally. "This is how I am."

"I missed you, too," Karen said.

We walked to the baggage chute holding hands.

I said, "We're never going to be apart this long again."

At The Lodge, my mother embraced Karen warmly. They sat on

adjacent wicker chairs in front of the fireplace. Karen asked about my mom's split-second decision to fly to South Lake Tahoe. This led to talk about lengthy Alaska winters, and Mom's working the salmon season in the cafeteria at the cannery where Del previously worked.

I distributed hot tea. I sat on the green couch mostly as a spectator.

Mom asked about Karen's visit, and her family. Karen described growing up Back East, as Westerners say. She didn't boast about her famous grandfather, Clyde Tuohy Whitney, godfather of satellite weather technology. She didn't toss a hint about family money. Karen conversed more easily with my mother than I did.

Mom said, "Sounds like everybody gets along."

Karen said, "Except Aunty Rae. Even though she tends to be a problem, it seemed only fair to invite her to a family reunion. She lasted two nights."

"What happened?"

"You'd have to know Aunty Rae." Karen turned to me. "Jeff's met her. How would you describe?"

"She looks for an argument where there isn't one. She wants more than her fair share of family resources."

Karen flashed perfect teeth. "I think we can move on."

I'd noticed a coat slung over a dining table chair. When she and Karen's talking wound down, Mom stood and announced she was going to the movies.

"I'll make it a double feature," she said.

Karen and Mom hugged. Mom hugged me, grabbed her coat and left. She waved goodbye behind her. The door shut.

Karen said, "You made her out to be a country bumpkin. She's terrific."

"It's... complicated."

Karen and I, after more than two weeks on opposite sides of the country, were alone in a large cabin on a picturesque alpine lake. The view across the water and to far off Freedom Peak was enchanting. We went to the bedroom. I lighted two burgundy candles. Their glow made quivering halos on the pine ceiling. We undressed each other. We went under the blankets and kissed. We kissed some more.

We brought each other up pleasure mountains. White lights exploded in my head.

In the morning, Karen went to Barton Memorial Hospital to meet with who would be her coworkers beginning October first. Mom said she was going exploring in Nevada. I studied with more urgency, knowing prep time was running short.

Elise called. She invited the three of us to Mixx, dinner at eight.

"I know it's last minute. But it's a celebration for Karen's return and your mom's visit."

I went back to studying for the most important series of tests I'd ever take. Later, when Karen, Mom and I were together, I relayed the dinner party offer.

Karen said, "No thanks. I looked up Elise Jansen. She exists in another universe."

"She doesn't. You'd be surprised by how different she looks in person. How unpretentious she is."

Mom said, "I'm in. I've never been invited to dinner by a supermodel."

Karen looked to me. "Taylor?"

"Elise is lonely. Even separated, she and Brett were each other's daily connection to the world. Elise associates me with when Brett was healthy. She wants to be reminded of it. Besides, if we say no, it'll seem like her looks scare you off."

"Maybe they do."

Mom said, "I'm going, with or without you two. You said eight o'clock. Give me an address. I'll use the GPS."

"I guess that settles that," Karen said.

Mom said, "It'll be fun. At least interesting."

I gave warning about the upscale atmosphere at Mixx. Showers, then best clothes were donned. Driving away from Fallen Leaf Lake and down the highway, the fresh coldness of night seeping through windows, it felt like embarking on an adventure.

At Mixx, I spied Elise's beat-up Mercedes in the parking lot. We walked under the canvas entrance overhang, past strings of white lights. I opened the door. Mom entered first.

Maryanne, in a different little black dress than last time, greeted us. "Mrs. Boyd is seated." Maryanne led the way. That night her shiny dark hair swathed bare shoulders.

We passed well-heeled diners at tables with pure white tablecloths drifting over their ends. The diners reminded me of squeaky clean characters in a TV soap opera.

Mom glanced back over a shoulder. She whispered, "Fancy."

Elise rose to greet us. She sat in the same spot as our time there before. Introductions were not followed by swift cheek kisses. I attributed this to Karen's presence. Statuesque Elise wore an expansive pantsuit that looked like it required several yards of purple satin to create. Its sleeves draped to below her elbows.

Elise motioned for us to be seated. Her right hand pointed upward. The trim, dapper man with a silver goatee, in white coat and red bow tie, wheeled the silver cart, this night bearing four cocktail glasses.

He said, "Good evening, Mrs. Boyd." Nodding to me, he said, "Welcome back, sir." Then to Karen and Mom, "First time guests, I trust these will not disappoint."

Cocktails were distributed. The man bowed and wheeled the cart away.

Mom said, "Now that's service."

Elise looked to Karen. She recited my mom's words of three days prior. "It's nice to finally have a face to put the name to."

Mom floated a subtle wink in Elise's direction.

Karen said, "Elise, may I ask a question? About your name?"

I said, "That's personal."

Mom said, "Overruled." She downed a sip of her gimlet and watched Elise and Karen.

Karen said, "Thank you, your honor."

"What about it?" Elise said.

"Elise Jansen. It's perfect. Is modeling like acting, you make up a name if the one you're born with doesn't sound right?"

I said, "C'mon. We're her guests."

Elise beamed. "No worries, Boy Scout."

Karen said, "Boy Scout?"

"It's a nickname," I said.

Karen's eyes took a lap around the table. "I'm gone a couple weeks and my husband has a new name?"

Elise rotated her palms up. She rested bare forearms on both sides of a white plate. "My birth name is Dorothy Turnut." Elise made a fist of her right hand. She poised it like a microphone. "Now showing Versace's latest junk, give it up for Dorothy Turnut."

The joke loosened us up. Maryanne brought menus.

I said, "Was the name Annabee's doing?"

"Made me a lot of money over the years."

Karen said, "Who's Annabee? Is it another made-up name?"

"Her Honor demands to know who Annabee is."

Elise said, "May I offer a story?"

"Damn right you can," Mom said.

"I'm in line at Westwood Cinemas. Night. Bright lights. A red carpet longer than a bowling lane. Me and a girlfriend are waiting for the premiere of *Falling Home*."

Mom said, "I love that movie. It's great when—"

"Mom, it's her story."

"Sorry."

Elise flipped a hand in my direction, telling me it was okay. "We're looking down the red carpet, waiting for the actors and the director to show. A limo pulls up. I'm watching the driver open the back door when my arm gets tapped." Elise tapped her left forearm. "A deep voice says, 'Come see me. We got work to do.' I look over. A woman dressed in a red coat, red tie and red slacks presses her business card in my hand, and walks away. Annabee Flowers. That's how I got into modeling."

The man in the bow tie began his floor voyage. Karen and Mom watched him like an actor in a play that he was. The man arrived. Mom shook her head.

"No, thank you."

"As you wish. I brought water for all."

Mom said, "You kids get plowed. I'll be the designated driver."

Elise said, "Who's going to drive me home?"

"See if you can leave your car," Mom said. "It'll be like when Jeffy first played sports. I'd pack my Ford wagon with kids, drive 'em up and down the coast."

Karen said, "Jeffy?"

"It's another nickname," I said.

Elise raised a hand. "That's so sweet." Maryanne appeared, seemingly out of nowhere. Elise handed her a car key. "Put my car in back. I'll come for it in the morning."

Round three of gimlets arrived. Someone decided we'd all have fillet of Tahoe Mackinaw Trout. The fish arrived on beds of romaine lettuce with Maine scallops arranged around them, and steaming vegetables. Nourished by good food and drink, for a while it seemed like our bubbly table was the only one in the restaurant, that we had the whole place to ourselves. At times everyone talked at once. It was that kind of night.

The woman in a white tuxedo plunked standards on the grand piano. Drink number four arrived. Elise shook her head when Maryanne asked if we wanted dessert. We stumbled out into cheeks-stinging night air. Mom got behind the wheel. We were off.

Mom went straight upstairs to sleep. Karen and I wandered downstairs in a boozy haze. We drank water.

Inebriated Karen said, "She's not stunning, like her pictures. But there's something about her. You just want to look. You just want to look at her."

In the morning we drifted into the great room. The kitchen smelled of cooked oatmeal. Karen found a note on the dining area table.

Jeff and Karen,

Thank you for the hospitality. I arrived without warning and you both welcomed me. Now I need to see my parents, who I haven't seen in more years than I want to admit. As you know, we had a parting of the ways when I got pregnant at 19. They are getting on in years. I should see them. After that, I plan on going to Grantsville. At first life there was lonely but we got to know people and it was a big chunk of my life. Whenever it is I go back to Alaska, I plan to return to South Lake Tahoe and fly from there/here.

Love, Mom to you both

PART TWO

Fifteen

Karen began work the next week, supervising half a floor in the seniors care unit at Barton Memorial Hospital. I shifted my preparation for the state medical exams into overdrive.

Brett and Elise took a backseat in my mind. That ended when, after a pre-dinner jog and shower, I walked into the great room wearing a T-shirt, Jockey shorts, socks on the cool wood floor—and saw Karen from behind. Her arms wrapped around a weeping Elise. Elise's sobs were not loud, but they were steady. Karen rocked her in a way suggestive of two people slow dancing.

Elise said, "I know I shouldn't have come. I couldn't face being alone."

I hurried to the bedroom and slipped on a pair of jeans. I came back out. Karen walked Elise to one of the wicker chairs covered with cushions the same dark green as the cushions on the long couch. Elise sat and stared at seemingly nothing. Karen patted her shoulder, went to the kitchen.

I said, "What happened?"

Elise shook her head. "I know I shouldn't have come."

"No need to think like that."

Karen returned with a blue cloth napkin. "You're welcome here any time."

I sat across from Elise. She looked much like when we'd met for the first time, at her place: disheveled hair, puffy face. Karen placed the cloth napkin in her hands. Elise wiped her face.

Karen said, "The county released Brett's ashes today. Elise went to spread them at Sky Lake. It knocked her off stride."

Elise wiped her nose. She shuddered. "It was going fine. I walked the shore, spilling ashes in the water. Talking to Brett. There was a knot in my chest, but spreading his ashes and talking was breaking it up. I made the mistake of looking behind me, at what's left of the house. We loved that place. It was our escape until things got too crazy. I threw the last ashes in and ran to the car."

"I get it," I said.

Elise looked up, found me. "I didn't come just because I'm upset. I thought of somebody who was angry enough at me to—I don't know—but used to be angry enough he could do something violent."

She had my attention. "Who?"

Karen stepped away from Elise, and looked at her more intently.

Elise said, "David Gummer. I didn't think of him. It's been a long time. But he's the only person I can think of who might want to harm Brett."

"No matter how unlikely, tell us," I said.

Elise gave her nose another pass with the blue napkin. "David and I were a couple the night Brett came into my life." Her eyes met mine. "He did PR for the shows. He went batshit when I left him. Sent emails saying he was going to break Brett's legs, so he'd never ski again. Stuff like that. Then, like two years ago—"

"If you could find those emails, it would be helpful."

Karen shot me a look that meant *don't interrupt.*

Elise said, "About two years ago, Hooly—Abilene Houlihan, one of the mods—texted me she heard David's in Reno."

I looked to Karen. "Mods means one of the models."

Karen nodded.

Elise said, "I'd told Hooly things with Brett were a mess. I'm sure she was trying to help. I don't even know if David's still in Reno."

I said, "Are you afraid of him?"

Elise's fingers went to her mouth. "I think I always was. I hate to admit it, but he was the kind of bad boy I used to like to run with." She raked hands back through blonde hair, pursed her lips. "He'd shift from party mode to punching somebody in like a second."

Elise described Gummer, his background, his part in rolling out the shows. She asked if she could clean up in a bathroom. When Elise emerged, like the first time we'd met, she was transformed. She thanked us. Karen and I walked Elise to her car and received fluttery double cheek kisses.

Elise drove off. Behind her rose brown dust consisting of crushed pine needles. I turned to Karen, who nibbled at the tip of her ponytail.

She said, "Don't you even think about going to Reno until after the boards."

The day before the state boards began, I took a room at a hotel in a quiet Sacramento neighborhood. For the next two days I poured years of study into the various sections of the state medical exam. Then I called Clint Sherman, my old boss at Sherman Investigations, and invited him to dinner at Clint's favorite restaurant, Frank Fat's. Clint's eighty years showed more than I remembered from the last time I'd seen him, only eight weeks before. His gait had become nearly a shuffle. At Frank Fat's we talked more about Brett's death than the state boards.

Upon parting, Clint said, "David Gummer. Last known address, Reno."

I drove home to South Lake Tahoe and searched for what I could find out about Gummer. Clint located the same Reno addresses, home and business, as I did. He also found court records in Miami, New York and Los Angeles for aggravated assault. They all involved fights over women Gummer had previously dated. In Los Angeles he'd beaten a man with an aluminum baseball bat and served forty-five days. I called Elise and relayed this to her.

"None of it surprises me," she said. "I knew about Miami because I was there."

I kissed Karen on the cheek and wished her a good day at work.

She said, "Reno?"

"I'm not staying away from a possible connection to Brett's death, no matter how slight. That's not going to happen."

"It's stubborn mule time, huh? When you get like this, you're impossible."

"So you admit it's inevitable?"

"I admit you can be a jackass."

"I love you, too."

Downtown Reno sported a mix of modern cement and glass skyscrapers, old single-story casinos, used clothing stores and hip bistros. Thick traffic. Gummer's public relations company, DG Solutions, resided on the third floor of a steel building that shimmered under desert sun. The suite consisted of one large room with a slick glass desk at its back center. A separate desk, oak with right-side drawers, accommodated a laptop. Two walls were lined with framed color photographs of clients. The floor was polished cement.

I knew Gummer's age, forty-three. The internet photos I'd found from his days on the modeling circuit prepared me to meet a fit, tan man who was light on his feet. The David Gummer I met was all that. His hair was a rich brown, tousled in a way that seemed the product of effort. He had dark pouches below hazel eyes that seemed a little sad to me. His skin reminded me of a lizard's. Perhaps the desert sun had baked that into him. He didn't have a scar in and above his right eyebrow.

Gummer's handshake was vigorous. Tan blazer and slacks gave the appearance of someone who was trying hard to look cool. Still, a forthright sincerity came with the salesman's persona.

We exchanged names. Gummer gestured for me to sit in a polished mahogany chair. He sat behind the glass desk in a plush chair with wheels.

"What line of work are you in?"

"I'm a physician."

Gummer smiled. His teeth were bleached as pale a white as roadside bones you pass on isolated country roads. "Do you know of our work involving medical practices? We've managed half a dozen launchings." He pointed to pictures on the wall. "Take a look. I'll talk you through any you want."

I got up and found a photo of a highway billboard advertising an orthodontics practice. "I don't want to mislead you. I'm not here for a PR campaign."

"Oh? What can I help you with?"

"I'd like to talk to you about what happened with Brett Boyd."

"Brett? Last I heard, he quit skiing to become a full-time nothing. I'm not in regular communication with people from my past. What has he got himself into?"

"He got himself into getting killed."

Gummer's face froze. "Skiing stoned? Drunk driving?"

"He was murdered."

I described Brett's death and the role a silver-plated belt buckle played in it. I told Gummer that Brett's chalet and garage had burned to the ground.

"The fire department says arson. You sure you didn't know about Brett's passing?"

I'd come for precisely that moment, to look for reactions that hinted at Gummer's involvement. The more I talked, the quicker Gummer recovered from hearing about Brett's death.

"Well," he said, "the bastard finally got what he deserved. I don't know why you're here, but you bring good news. Are you some kind of cop?"

"Brett and I were friends growing up."

He stood, kind of rolled his shoulders and continued to display the roadside bones teeth. "What are you doing, going around spreading the good news?"

A sensation, like rising steam, rose in my head. It came with heat and buzzing in my ears.

"I'm looking into how he died. His wife says it's possible you're grinding an old axe against him. Against her and him both."

"You know Elise? Who cheated on me, who dumped me for no reason?"

I nodded.

What seemed pent-up anger flashed in red patches across Gummer's face. "Is she your pussy now?"

I crossed the room and slapped Gummer's face as hard as I could. He staggered sideways.

His tone defiant, Gummer said, "Best piece ever."

I struck Gummer with a roundhouse punch that knocked him over like a bowling pin. My words hissed like the steam in my head. "Put a cork in it. *Now.*"

An air conditioner hummed. Outside, a horn honked. Looking down at Gummer, I waited. It was his move.

He wiped his mouth, checked for blood. "Okay." His face and neck scarlet, Gummer clutched the armrest of his chair. He grunted and, after rolling the chair toward him, worked his way to his feet and sat.

I returned to the mahogany chair.

Gummer positioned himself behind the desk again. He looked through the glass for quite a while before speaking. "Elise and I went to this party at the ocean. It was wild. They were all wild. The time to go comes, and some makeup guy tells me Elise left with somebody else. Like an hour before. Completely out of the blue, we're over."

"It must've been quite a shock."

Gummer looked at me. "Not that many years ago, I would've gotten up and knocked you on your ass."

"I don't doubt it," I lied.

My body downshifted. Adrenaline topped off, receded.

Gummer said, "I was out of my mind in love with her. Nutso in love with her. Does she have you like that?"

"No."

"I think she does. That's why you hit me. Elise is like dope. You get hooked. It's all you want. It took me two years to get my head back on straight. I came here on the advice of a friend, to get away from that whole world. I'm with a good woman named Gale now."

"I'm happy to hear it."

Gummer rubbed his jaw. His face still flushed, he said, "I made those cracks about Elise because I think I still love her. After five years. Hell, I know I'm still in love with her. I can't stop it."

Gummer re-knotted his tan tie. He reached to the bottom right drawer beneath the glass desk. Through the clear tabletop I saw the drawer open. I watched this closely. Rather than a weapon, Gummer took out a bottle of Dewar's. He placed the Scotch on the see-through desk. Reaching farther into the drawer, Gummer withdrew two shot glasses. He offered me a drink.

"You go ahead. I've got to drive back to Fallen Leaf Lake."

Gummer poured himself a shot. He downed it with a practiced flick of his wrist. "Fallen Leaf? Gale and I go there all the time in summer. To get away from Reno heat. She has a tent trailer we take to the campground."

Gummer poured himself a second round, swirled the liquor, threw it down. His gaze stayed on the glass between us. He didn't speak.

Gummer poured himself a third swig of Scotch.

I said, "Could I take a look at that bottle?"

This seemed to wake him up. "Whatever."

Gummer slid the bottle and the empty shot glass forward. I secured the bottle and headed for the door.

Gummer snapped, "What the hell you think you're doing?"

I stopped. "I know your address. You live a dozen miles from here. It's eleven in the morning. You want to get home without incident."

"Go to hell."

I opened the door. I heard Gummer's chair roll. He took steps toward me. His hands disappeared in pockets of the tan slacks. He grinned. It was a weak grin, almost an apologetic grin. "Will you tell her? Will you tell Elise I still think about her? Tell her I think about her a lot."

"I'll tell her you wish her the best."

"I do wish her the best. Don't you forget it. Now get out of here before I lose my temper."

On the way to my car I dumped the Scotch in a garbage can. The bottle thudded at hitting bottom.

Sixteen

I left hot and crowded Reno. I drove up the Mt. Rose Highway. Coming down, my phone jingled. I turned into the parking lot at the overlook station. Gazing south, Lake Tahoe seemed even larger than it had from the summit of Mt. Tallac. I gaped at its profound beauty while answering the phone.

Jim Stevens said, "Tell me again about your two times tailing the suspect. Don't skip anything."

"Okay. First time was during the day. I followed him almost to Kirkwood. He cut down a seldom-used road, parked at a former ski resort. Fired two shots from somewhere unknown. I got out of there fast. The second time was at night, from the restaurant Antonio's. That time he went into Kirkwood. I didn't follow because he could've trapped me in there. What's this all about?"

"So you never actually went into Kirkwood. Or saw the suspect outside a particular building, right?"

"That is correct."

"Does the name Gary Fingler mean anything to you?"

"He came in second in the tournament."

"The sicko struck again."

My stomach clenched. I stared ahead but didn't take in the view of the lake. The pavement in front of me seemed to heave, like there was an earthquake.

"Jeff? You there?"

"Yeah."

"He got Fingler at his condo in Kirkwood Village. Where you said you thought the suspect was staying. He must have been scouting his next victim. You sure you didn't see where he went in Kirkwood?"

"Goddamn it, of course I'm sure. I already told you. I didn't follow him in because I could've gotten trapped." I flung open the car door and paced the lot. "The same belt buckle thing?"

"Yes. I was operating under the assumption somebody killed Brett, then went after me because the paper cited me as in charge of the investigation. I never considered other potential victims."

"You have the names of all the contestants?"

"Two deputies are contacting them right now."

"I remember reading the winner is from Tahoe City."

"That's Placer County. I already got hold of Sheriff Reynolds. He's going to La Porte's business as we speak. Plus a voice message was left telling La Porte not to open any packages. Any packages arrive, he calls the police."

I paced. "Now don't get pissed, but I want to remind you he returned to the scene after he got Brett."

"Kirkwood is Amador County. They already have Fingler's place staked out."

"I didn't mean to insult you."

"You didn't. And you and I didn't have this conversation. You got that? It's not yet decided what to tell the papers. If you come across anything in your freelancing, call me pronto."

"Will do."

"One more thing. I heard from Pat Davis about belt buckles. Early August, five were shipped to a private mail center in Fresno. Buyer sent cash for them."

"What's his name?"

"The name he used was Brett Boyd. They're not strict about I.D. at this place. Fresno P.D. say it's shady, but legal."

"The son of a bitch."

Stevens hung up. I wandered in the parking lot. A car rolled in. The man driving honked and shook his head at me for blocking the middle of the driving lane. I'd had nothing to do with Brett's death, or Fingler's, or the attempt on Stevens' life, yet considered myself fully involved. To be aware of evil going on and doing nothing about it was not acceptable to me.

At The Lodge I made dinner for Karen since she was the employed person of the house. She came home to one of my mediocre meals of turkey burgers and broccoli, with sliced avocado on crackers as an appetizer. I told Karen about my time in Reno, leaving out smacking Gummer twice. I told her about Stevens' call informing me of Gary Fingler's murder.

Karen said, "I hate it when you get like this. Catch the guy, okay? Then we can get back to what we came here for."

I didn't offer a comment. I reflected on how, in little more than two weeks, I was hiding three incidents from Karen: stretching out on the blanket with Elise at Cradle Lake; getting a hand massage from Elise on the couch in The Lodge when my mom popped in; hitting Gummer.

I caught myself. There were so many, I'd missed one: two gunshots at the abandoned ski resort.

Dishes were done, the fire relighted. We settled in for a cozy night where the backdrop was not music but the musical popping of sticky pitch and low flames, and the smell of woodsmoke. My phone pinged. I picked it up. For the first time I had a negative reaction at seeing Elise's name.

"Hello."

She whispered, "He's here. He thinks I'm going pee."

I hopped to my feet, alarming Karen such that she did the same. "*Shit.* The guy we think did it?"

"David. He showed up, banging on the door. Drunk out of his mind."

"Why'd you let him in?"

"He's a mess. He's… If you saw him, you'd understand. He's crying his eyes out. Can you help? I left the front door unlocked."

I hadn't informed Elise about my trip to Reno.

"When I hang up, call 911. Give them your address. Tell them someone uninvited and unarmed is in your house. He's unarmed, right?"

"I'm sure of it. He never carried a gun. He's mostly helpless."

"Be sure to tell 911 he's not armed. You got that?"

Karen's eyes sizzled. She pointed at my phone, wanting information.

Elise said, "What David says is true. I dumped him without warning. I just walked away with Brett and never gave David a reason. It was cruel and selfish. Should I tell the police any of that?"

"I changed my mind. Don't call 911. I'm coming over." I hung up and met Karen's gaze. "That guy I saw in Reno today? Elise's ex boyfriend? He just showed up. I should go."

"Follow your advice. Call 911 and give them her address."

I lifted a sweatshirt off the back of a chair. "If she calls 911 and Jim Stevens hears it, on dispatch, he'll go play protector and maybe do damage to the guy. He could rough him up, to show off, and the guy's just drunk."

Karen said, "I don't get it."

"Stevens is nuts about Elise."

"I think you're all nuts about Elise."

Karen walked to the downstairs hallway. I heard a door shut. I patted the pockets of my jeans, felt keys and headed out. At the one break in forest on the way to the highway, a large meadow, stars rained light that glittered on the dark grass like diamonds.

Parked crookedly in Elise's double driveway, the front of a new-looking red Ford Expedition glistened under floodlights. Gummer had stopped two feet short of ramming the garage door. I told myself to slow down, to act physically only on defense. I opened the door, stepped in. Whimpering came from the living room. Entering it I saw an empty bottle of Dewar's on its side on the beige carpet.

Elise sat on the shiny leather couch. Gummer was on his knees, at her feet.

He said, "If you come back, we can go anywhere you want. Anywhere on earth."

Elise patted Gummer's tousled hair as if she were petting a dog.

He said, "I need you."

"The problem," I said, "is she doesn't need you."

Gummer looked up. Bloodshot eyes and strain reddened his face. A blast of energy shot through his drunken body.

"So I was right," he said. "You're seeing her, you cheap-shot bastard."

Gummer struggled to get up. He staggered toward me. He let out a rumbling sound and took a swing. I stepped aside like a matador. Gummer tumbled to the carpet.

He attempted to rise. I pushed him down. He got to his knees. I pushed him down again. Gummer looked around as if unsure of where he was. He wore the tan slacks and white shirt of the morning. The blazer and tie were gone.

I said, "Give me your keys."

He shook his head.

"You drive in your condition, you'll either kill somebody or kill yourself."

I stood over him, looked to Elise. She mouthed *sorry*.

Gummer seemed to have caught up to a thought. "Were you two together, before Brett went down?"

Elise said, "Shut up. You're just drunk."

"You bolted on me. Maybe you did it again."

I said, "I'll say it once. Elise and I aren't seeing each other. The only reason I'm here is she wouldn't call the police on you. She's doing you a favor."

Gummer tried to sit up. He couldn't, and instead curled onto a side. His white shirt, untucked, had a stain at its center. He smelled strongly of whiskey. "I just need a few minutes."

"You have one minute. Then you're giving me your keys and we're out of here."

As if surrendering, Gummer closed his eyes and let his head rest on the carpet. Exhausted, he breathed heavily. Gummer fell into a wheezing sleep. I looked to Elise. She rounded all the way forward, squeezed her knees. I considered walking out on both of them.

After a couple of minutes, I bent down and slapped Gummer's cheek.

He woke up and pissed his pants. He looked at the dark spot on his slacks.

I said, "Your car keys. It's either me or the police."

The slap seemed to revive him. Gummer worked fingers into the right front pocket of the tan slacks, extracted keys and rose his arm.

I pocketed the keys. "Let's go. We're going to keep you safe."

Gummer looked to Elise. It was as if he'd woken from a protracted, bewildering dream. Gummer said, "I can be better. I know I can be better."

Elise turned away from him.

I said, "I'm going to walk you to your car."

Gummer said, "How'd you get here?"

"Elise called me instead of the police. Like I told you."

"The police?"

I yanked Gummer to his feet, took an arm and guided him to the front door. I opened the door with my free hand. Gummer stumbled toward my Subaru. I rerouted him and packed Gummer into the glossy red Ford Expedition. I went around and got in the driver's seat.

I said, "Put your seatbelt on."

The Expedition's new car smell mingled with the smell of alcohol. I went along Pioneer Trail toward Lake Tahoe.

I said, "How'd you know where Elise lives?"

"Made a few calls. One of them knew who to ask."

"Someone who thinks you were better for Elise than Brett?"

Gummer closed his eyes. "More like someone who likes to stir shit up. Those people," Gummer said, "are mostly skinny pieces of crap."

Pioneer Trail led us to downtown South Lake Tahoe. Eight p.m., traffic was steady with people going to and coming from casinos. Signs flashed at motels on every block.

Gummer said, "Where you taking me?"

"Somewhere you can sleep it off."

"If I weren't drunk, I'd knock you on your ass."

I turned into a driveway at a motel called El Rancho. I told Gummer to stay put. He closed his eyes and rested back against the seat. In the knotty pine motel office, I explained to the night clerk that my passenger was too drunk to drive. The office window gave view of the parked Expedition. I looked over in case Gummer tried to make a run for it. I paid, and said I'd return in the morning to drop off Gummer's keys.

I felt no adrenaline, no satisfaction. I was doing a job that needed doing, nothing more. Back in the car, I headed down the parking lane. The Expedition rolled slowly over a speed bump. I turned into the parking space for room twenty-four. I gave Gummer the room key card and motioned for him to get out.

"You can pick up your keys at the office, any time after eight in the morning. Now get some sleep."

Gummer said, "You made me look bad in front of Elise. You're going to pay for it. Hear me, cheap-shot bastard? You're gonna pay."

Seventeen

Gummer's Expedition was at the motel before eight a.m. I texted for an Uber. When the driver turned into Elise's court lined with pine trees, I had him stop, paid with the app and told him to turn around and leave quietly. The driver gave me a funny look but didn't ask why. I walked to a light-colored sedan parked facing to exit the court, not directly in front of a house. No pine needles littered its roof. I walked toward Elise's house. Well ahead, a man scurried between trees. He went to a window and peered inside. A camera rose to eye level.

I phoned Elise.

She said, "I owe you one for last night. Coming for your car?"

"You might have visitors in a minute. Me and a guest. If you could have the door unlocked, like last night, it would be helpful."

"I don't think I like this."

"Not to worry. Please unlock the front door."

I crossed the street and tucked behind pickups and tree trunks. Unlike with Gummer, my pulse beat faster. The man with fluffy hair over his ears went from one downstairs window to the next. The same dark overcoat, slacks and black hard shoes as at Taylor Creek. I moved swiftly. I re-crossed the street at an angle that put me between him and the parked sedan. Then sprinted. He heard foot falls, turned and tried to outflank me. I bear hugged him,

143

backed him to the wood siding of the house, secured the lapels of his sports coat and bounced him off the wall. He dropped a small camera.

"Chris Cranston?"

Squinting, frightened, he nodded. "Yeah."

"Why are you looking in house windows at eight in the morning?"

I bounced him off the house again, which shook his fluffy hair. He grunted in pain, and sagged. I grabbed his coat again, hoisted and spun him around, snatched a wallet from a back pocket of his slacks. I slipped the wallet away, pushed the man to the front door, opened it and shoved him hard.

I said, "Come on in. No need to sneak around."

"I don't know what you're talking about."

I marched him to the living room, pushed him onto the leather couch.

"Stay put. You'd never beat me to your car."

The man looked around at the paintings, sculptures and polished teak bookcases.

Elise entered the room.

I sat in an easy chair. "Remember Chris Crawford? From watching the salmon? Today he goes by Chris Cranston."

Elise said, "How interesting."

She sat in the other russet easy chair. The man who called himself Chris continued to look around.

Finally, he spoke. "I'm going to call the police."

"I have a direct number to one of the officers," I said. "You want it? Make sure you tell him I caught you looking in bedroom windows."

Elise said, "If you left your phone at the newspaper, you're welcome to use mine."

The man returned to his visual inventory.

I said to Elise, "I found a wallet by your front door. Let's see who it belongs to."

The man who called himself Chris said, "You just can't knock someone around like that."

Elise said, "I didn't see him knock you around. Jeff, did you knock him around?"

"Last time we crossed paths, he made up a fake name. What's to stop him from making that up?"

I opened the wallet and read from the driver's license. "Harold O'Rourke." I turned to Elise. "This wallet belongs to Harold O'Rourke. Do you know a Harold O'Rourke?"

Elise feigned trying to recall if she did. She touched the back of her right hand to her forehead, and frowned as if deep in thought. Her years on runways likely contributed to her acting style, which while melodramatic was good enough for the moment at hand. Elise said, "I don't know anyone with that name." She looked to the man on the couch. "Do you know anyone named Harold O'Rourke?"

He didn't answer.

I plucked a business card from the wallet. "Harold's card says he's a forensic investigator. Sounds like serious stuff." I read from the card. "All forms of insurance fraud, corporate and private."

O'Rourke swallowed over tautness showing on his face. "Could I have a glass of water?"

Elise said, "Sure. Jeff, you want anything?"

"No thanks."

Elise rose. She traversed the beige carpet. O'Rourke watched her walk to the kitchen area as if appraising her. He looked out the sliding glass door. Its curtains were drawn open. "Did you sneak around the back?"

"Unlike you," I said, "I didn't sneak anywhere."

"But your car's here."

"You know what's more interesting than where I left my car last night? Insurance fraud. Let's talk about insurance fraud."

Elise re-entered the living room. She handed O'Rourke a glass of water. He took a quick sip.

Elise said, "I'd like to learn about insurance fraud. But if you want to call the police first, that's okay with me."

O'Rourke finished the water, carefully set the glass on a side table, checking to be sure it didn't leave a water mark. He stood.

"Do you mind if I take off my coat?"

Elise said, "*Mi casa* is your *casa*. Or something like that."

The insurance investigator regained composure. "I have a pen and notebook in the car. If we're going to talk, I'll need 'em for notes."

I said, "Give your memory a workout."

Elise said, "I can fix this. Be right back."

Elise exited the room.

O'Rourke said, "It must be hard being her boyfriend. Men checking her out all the time."

I didn't bother trying to explain I wasn't Elise's boyfriend. She returned to the living area, handed O'Rourke a pen and notebook.

Elise said, "If you need anything else, just let me know."

"How about if we go to that dining table over there? We'll chat, I'll make notes. Let's see if we can learn from each other."

"While you two settle in," I said, "I'll pop outside and get you your camera."

"That would be great."

Elise said, "If you keep looking at me the way you've been, I'll have Jeff break your nose. Kick your ass from here to Nevada."

O'Rourke flinched. Then shivered. I went outside. I stifled an urge to laugh. The little camera was metal. I picked it up and removed the CompactFlash Card containing images. I went back inside. Crossing the large living area, I waved the camera.

"Here you go." I set it in front of Harold O'Rourke. Before sitting down, I stepped back, whipped out my phone and took a picture of him sitting at the table with his camera and Elise.

He said, "What's that for?"

"Evidence you were here. That you brought your camera. In case we end up with the police, and I tell them you were looking in bedroom windows."

O'Rourke made squiggly lines on the first notebook page. "Let's get down to business."

Sitting across from Elise and me at the table, O'Rourke gave us an introduction to his line of work. He exhibited an evident pride.

"I receive a modest fee up front, plus expenses. I get a percentage of what I save the company if I produce something that makes it so they don't have to pay the beneficiary. That's where it can get lucrative."

I said, "Brett's life insurance is a lot of money to avoid paying."

O'Rourke graced the table with one of his easy smiles. "I've obtained both cases. Death and fires." He made a few more squiggles with the pen. "There is an array of possible causes for nonpayment. I'll cover what's relevant here. If the beneficiary was materially responsible for death, the company doesn't have to pay. There is a no payment clause in case of suicide, based on Mr. Boyd's behavioral history. With the fires, if it was arson, and the beneficiary caused the fire, the company doesn't have to pay. This is all really a matter of keeping people honest."

Elise rubbed fingertips in a circle on her forehead. "Let me get this straight. You're investigating me for possibly killing Brett, then burning down the house?"

"That's right. If it turns out to be the case, or if you instructed an accomplice," O'Rourke said, tipping his head at me, "the company doesn't have to pay."

Elise went to the kitchen. She propped herself against a white tile counter. "Listen. I don't think I could get this Boy Scout to cheat on his wife, let alone kill somebody and burn down a house. Brett and I loved that place. It was our sanctuary from me at the shows and him at the tournaments. You know Brett was a former world champion water skier, right?"

"Ms. Jansen, I probably know as much about Brett Boyd as you do."

Elise pushed herself off the counter. Her eyes shot blue light into the dining area. "You don't know shit about Brett. You have addresses, news stories, maybe knowledge of his finances. But you don't know shit about Brett Boyd."

"There's no need to argue the point. I'll tell you, though, I'm sure I know more about Jeff than you."

Elise stayed in the kitchen. "Congratulations. Now it's time for you to go."

I said, "Before he does, a couple of things. Why do you keep looking around, like a burglar casing the place?"

"When a beneficiary is guilty of trying to game the system, he or she often buys luxury items ahead of payment. Take that large painting over there. The mountain snow scene. How long have you had it? The frame, the whole thing looks new. Everything about it seems fresh on the wall."

Elise's voice boomed with coarseness: "Screw you! Go away."

I said, "I need to let him know a few things about what happened at Sky Lake."

Elise said, "Why not? It's my house, and everybody else gets to do exactly what they want."

O'Rourke said, "I know what happened at Sky Lake."

"We'll see," I said.

Elise stayed in the kitchen. She leaned a hip against the white tile counter.

I described my first encounter with the man wearing a yellow windbreaker, leaving out the pistol on his hip because I hadn't told Elise about it. I told O'Rourke about the man's looking for me at Antonio's and Blizzard Casino. I skipped the gunshots at the abandoned ski resort. I left out my interactions with Gummer, and Billy Whitmer. I didn't want to open any worm cans involving me for O'Rourke to sift through.

He asked questions and took notes. When I finished, he set the pen down, picked up the notebook, and stood. "Thank you. You were right. There are items I didn't know about. Now let's be clear. If you two haven't done anything illegal, you have nothing to worry about. If you have, eventually I'll root it out. What happens then is up to the courts."

I stood to say goodbye. Elise didn't leave the kitchen.

"I'll walk him to his car," I said, and motioned for O'Rourke to lead the way. He had the camera and notebook in one hand. He set them on the brown leather couch. He put on his dark sports coat. I handed over the wallet. We went outside into a cool gray morning and walked toward his car.

I said, "What have you gotten from South Tahoe police?"

"I avoid small town police departments as long as I'm able to. I've had experiences with them tipping off people they're friendly with."

"I assume you know the police investigation into Brett's death is headed by a Sergeant Stevens."

"Of course. A local boy. He'd be sympathetic to both of you. He might try to steer me off course."

No cars passed in either direction. It was strange how easy going,

149

even friendly, things were between us, considering O'Rourke was investigating me for possible accessory to murder, or murder, and arson.

I said, "You might ask Sergeant Stevens if he thinks Elise had anything to do with Brett's death. See what kind of reaction you get."

O'Rourke stopped walking. "Like I said, he's a local boy."

He put out his hand. He shook my half hand, and looked at it. "You should have sued that packing company. You could've gotten a million five. Maybe two. Didn't attorneys contact you?"

"About twenty. But it was my fault. I didn't follow procedure. I got sloppy and did exactly what I was warned against."

O'Rourke shook his head. "Now I've heard it all."

I took my hand back and patted O'Rourke on a shoulder. "May the gods have mercy on your poor, pathetic soul."

I walked back to Elise's. Tree branches swayed in the morning breeze. At reaching my car I felt a desire to get in and drive away. Instead, I went into the house. Elise cried and said she was tired of being scared.

Eighteen

I had a noon interview at Field Pediatrics, in South Lake Tahoe. After years of medical school, countless nights of studying past midnight, I'd nearly reached my lifelong goal of becoming a pediatrician. Yet driving back to The Lodge all I thought about was catching the man who killed Brett, and what photographs were on the CompactFlash card I'd taken from O'Rourke's camera.

The pictures contained no revelations. The scorched remains of the chalet and garage; my car and license plate; Elise's car and license plate; half a dozen shots of Elise and me at Taylor Creek; Elise's house from a few angles; the Subaru in front of Elise's house the night before. I deleted them all and tossed the CompactFlash Card in the trash.

Before moving to Fallen Leaf Lake, I'd researched pediatrics practices within driving distance. The practice of Margaret Field and Ron Hart stood out as a potential place of employment. Dr. Field was going into semi retirement. Hart coached most every type of youth sport; perhaps we'd be simpatico. And the practice was ten minutes from Karen's job at Barton Memorial. Sitting in the parking lot outside the office suite, I checked my tie and thinning brown hair in the car mirror. I decided to leave my briefcase.

Dr. Field, chatting with a parent in the reception area, welcomed me. She looked up through roundish glasses and shook my hand.

In her sixties, hair a silvery gray, Dr. Field's round face threw off a pleasant aura. "Follow me," she said, and opened a wood door. She wore a white lab coat and white jeans. We entered a conference room with windows facing the hallway. We made small talk about where I was living, how beautiful the area was, all that.

Dr. Hart popped in and shook hands. "Nice to meet you, but one of us is working today." He headed down the hallway.

Dr. Field said, "Call me Margaret. Call that comedian Ron. Staff refer to us more formally."

The interview covered what I expected. A surprise came when Margaret said that when filling a position she never contacted people who wrote letters of recommendation. "I go through the resume and make inquiries the candidate may not be prepared for. In your case, I saw you had a summer internship with a Dr. Fisher at the UC Med Center in Sacramento."

My attendance during the internship had been erratic. Heat prickled my forehead and the back of my neck.

I said, "Dr. Fisher has a way with patients I hope to emulate. He gets even three-year-olds to talk about what they're feeling."

I steadied myself for what might come next.

"He said it would be a mistake not to hire you before somebody else does."

"I'm flattered."

Considering the number of last-minute phone calls saying I wouldn't be in, I was stunned.

"One more question," Margaret said. "You were admitted to the program at UW, in Seattle. But you didn't attend. Didn't enter med school for four years. Were you having second thoughts about the profession?"

I lifted my right hand. "Not the profession. I worried—still do—I'll scare some of the patients."

"Jeff, if you were to join us, most patients with a disability, or a severe injury, would be assigned to you. Use that hand you don't seem to like to show children they can overcome anything."

Nineteen

Sitting on the back deck late Friday afternoon, Karen and I watched the sky soften, then darken. On the other side of Fallen Leaf Lake, beyond a stripe of forested ridge looming above the water, Freedom Peak glowed with the day's last light.

Karen said, "Let's climb Freedom tomorrow."

"Not possible. Even from here you can see how steep it is."

"I just want to get high enough we can look back this way. I don't think we'll see the lake, but it'd be fun to try."

I breathed pine-scented air. "I'm in."

Morning. We packed Karen's frayed green daypack. The drive took us on the same route I'd followed the black Range Rover twice. South into the wretched scars of the Kamen Fire. Left on Highway 89, climbing toward Luther Pass. As before, the terrain abruptly switched back to scenic high country splendor. I parked at a wide spot on the road's dirt shoulder behind a gray Toyota SUV and a dusty silver Honda Accord.

In matching orange Giants baseball caps, we ascended past trees and huge, black-pocked granite boulders. Carrying the day pack, I followed Karen. Her uphill strides came easily. She meshed with the glorious landscape; she was its equal. Above her, a robin's-egg-blue sky.

We met a party of two couples going downhill, and exchanged hellos.

The trail grew steep. We stopped for water at a place that gave view of Echo Summit. Far off, looking like ants, cars crawled over the pass and disappeared.

I slipped off the daypack, and sat. Karen offered the canteen. I drank and handed it back. Karen poured water onto one hand, splashed her face, then took a drink. At eight thousand feet up, the only animals about were pesky marmots that smelled either people or food in the daypack.

Karen joined me in sitting. "Elise is taking up too much space in our life."

I reached for the water, took another drink, spun the metal cap closed. "I agree."

"I should say Elise is taking up too much space in your life. Which is also my life."

"You know how I get. I won't be able to stop until whoever killed Brett is caught."

Karen pulled her ponytail to her lips. "No fancy talk. I was gone more than two weeks. Did you keep it in your pants? Yes or no?"

"That's not funny."

Karen said, "I'm not laughing. And you didn't answer."

"Because I'm insulted."

"Taylor, cut the crap. Even I'm attracted to her."

"You're attracted to Elise?"

"When she came over, after scattering Brett's ashes? She's crying. I give her a hug. We hold on for a while, and I wanted to kiss her. Like badly. I've never kissed a woman or even thought about it. So I can't help wondering about you. You two were together a lot. Are you attracted to her?"

"We didn't have sex. Period. I can't pretend she's not attractive."

Karen said, "More water."

She drank, handed back the metal canteen, stood, and slapped dust off her behind. Karen slid the pack on and motioned for me to start up the trail. We climbed. The thinness of the air became more notable. There were few trees—and they were scrawny.

I called back, "Are you really attracted to Elise? I'm jealous."

"*You're* jealous? When she called you Boy Scout, I wanted to kick her in the shins. It sounded intimate."

Karen sped up. She reached me. We halted. Karen looked me in the eyes.

I gulped water. I gave Karen the canteen. She gulped water.

Karen stepped forward and kissed me fully on the lips.

"What brought that on?"

"I don't know. Maybe Elise."

We resumed walking.

Above the tree line, we shared a quiet lunch. Quiet, that is, except for the hissing of wind scouring stone. The slope to Freedom Peak above us was so steep we lay back on rock and looked upon the earth as if from easy chairs. The earlier view of Echo Summit still hung in space, but it paled compared to looking down along the expansive Tahoe Basin and the colossal lake.

My mind turned off its endless radio. No voice played in my head. No images frolicked. No replaying snatches of a pop song. I felt completely refreshed, as if we hadn't slogged several miles uphill. Everything was seen with extraordinary clarity. I felt at peace with my surroundings.

Karen squeezed my shoulder. "You okay?"

"Better than okay."

We descended. Serenity stayed with me. At reaching forest, a slender trail wound its way downhill. The trees thickened. We passed small puddles amidst stands of Jeffrey pines. We stopped. We each took a swallow from the canteen.

Karen said, "Do you smell something? I think I smell something."

I said I didn't smell anything.

"I think it might be smoke," Karen said. Creasing her forehead in what I thought of as the family frown, thin brown eyebrows pulled together. "It's definitely smoke."

Off the trail, uphill, was a mound of granite as big as a house. "Maybe I can get a view."

It took hands as well as feet to scale the rock. I found a flat spot on top. Looking between trees, the sight provoked an involuntary string of profanities that was partly astonishment, partly fear. A mile away, a wall of orange flame consumed forest.

Karen looked up and shouted, "Fire?"

"Drop your pack. Get above the tree line."

Karen seemed puzzled.

"It's a fire. Go back!"

Karen slipped off the faded daypack. She looked up again. She shook her head *no*.

"Go! I'll catch up."

Propelled by the wind, clouds of black smoke rolled in our direction. A mile below, hundred-foot Jeffrey pines lighted like fourth of July sparklers. From that distance, watching the fire advance was like watching a silent movie. I felt a peculiar drunken pleasure.

Karen ceased heading up the trail. She motioned for me to get going. I threw my feet out, slid-bumped my way down stone. Seeing this, Karen ran uphill. I went to the daypack, took out a remaining plastic bottle of water and jammed it into a front pocket of my walking shorts.

I ran. Feet thumping the trail, trees blurred, the world bounced up and down. My mind churned faster than my legs. We couldn't crest the pass ahead of the blowing flames. It was too steep. We'd need to find a spot out of the wind. That would make it less likely flames blew across stone and burned us.

A raucous charge passed me. Deer raced by, and a red fox. A skunk scooted across the trail. Its backside waved back-and-forth frantically, like a fan. Last came a scurrying army of yellow-bellied marmots. Piercing alarm trills rang like a dozen kettles blasting steam. At seeing me they scattered in all directions.

I chased Karen uphill. We had a long way to go to get clear of vegetation.

A first wave of smoke arrived. It curled over my head. I breathed some in and coughed it out. Ahead, in smoky light, Karen looked like an apparition. I figured if we could get above the tree line we'd be inundated with smoke, and survive. The blanketing smoke was well ahead of the flames. At catching up with Karen, I squeezed her arm. Stitches of smoke-doused sunlight poked between trees.

I told myself: *Rocks don't burn.*

Adrenaline drove us up the slope. I tried to estimate how far it was to the tree line. I looked for landmarks and reminded myself to lift my feet with each step to avoid falling. The smoke thickened. We pressed on. The steepness of the trail, combined with the high-altitude air, slowed progress.

Heat radiated across the back of my neck, T-shirt and legs. With escalating horror I realized I'd vastly underestimated the speed of the blaze.

We ran for our lives.

To the left flames jumped from treetop to treetop like electric power lines springing to life. To our right, the same. Intense heat reached us as an undulating wave. Heat wrapped me in a kind of grip, further slowing me. Karen screamed and whipped her arms wildly. Flames shot everywhere.

"Jeff! Jeff!"

Karen cut rightward.

"Jeff!" She fell into a choking cough, which caused her to trip.

Bent over, coughing, slogging ahead, Karen called to me, "Here. Look here."

A high altitude remnant of the downpour on the day Elise and I had watched thrashing salmon, water and slushy snow pooled near the underside of a massive granite boulder. We scrambled up to it.

Karen went in on her back. She flipped her orange baseball cap aside. I stepped over her, sloshing water, to the boulder, seizing Karen's Giants cap on the way. I jammed it upside down where curving stone met damp earth. I set my phone on the baseball cap. Heat intensified.

Karen pulled at me.

I put my baseball cap atop the phone. The fire roared like jets firing up at an airport.

"Jeff! Now!"

I reached back with both hands and scooped mud, quick handfuls, and flung mud onto the baseball cap. Karen yanked me into the water. I came up spitting. Burning branches flashed all around us. Air was annihilated by fire.

I shouted over chaos. "Just lips out."

I worked my frame into the ground. Water barely covered us. Flames blasted our closed eyes with piercing orange light. It felt like the lid of a coffin closed over us. Between the flames and the water line, a shallow air pocket remained. Heat from passing flames sizzled my lips. I tasted blood. The water warmed like a bath.

I found Karen's hand. I began counting breaths. If I didn't breathe deeply the air pocket was clear enough of smoke I could inhale, exhale, stay steady.

Karen broke into coughing muffled by the fiery chaos. She ceased coughing. We aligned our bodies, making contact from feet to shoulders. Her body was warm.

The orange light grew familiar. Fear was accompanied by the

strange, yet comforting sounds of a music box. I was certain I'd heard those notes before. They had something to do with facing death. Had I burned to death before? No. Of course: I'd almost been drowned when facing off against a man who tried, and nearly succeeded, to kill me in a mountain stream years before. After that I'd quit being a detective.

Gradually, the orange light's density lessened, as did the chaotic sounds. The coffin lid slowly lifted. I opened my eyes, rose my head a few inches out of tepid water. Smoke hovered about four feet above the ground. Karen and I sat up in tandem.

The wake of the fire was a smoking, hissing jungle with small flames popping here and there. Raging wind had blown the flames by so fast most tree trunks were not burned. High above, their crowns flickered in smoke like individual torches.

Karen looked around. Her face appeared scratched all over. Her voice raspy, she said, "Your lips are bleeding."

"You, too."

Karen croaked, "I don't feel it. I don't feel anything."

My throat, constricted, burned as if a flare blazed inside it. Wind pushed black smoke in a steady stream those four feet above the ground.

Karen explored her bleeding lips, "What do we do?"

"If you hadn't seen this." I put a hand in the water. "If you hadn't seen this, we'd be gone." I sat up higher but kept my mouth low, away from the smoke. "Let's stay put. Ground will be burning all over."

"How long?"

"I don't know. I'll see if the phone works."

I crawled to the curved boulder. Mud balls covering the baseball cap baked my hand like taking biscuits from an oven. The cap was hot, as was the phone.

A few taps. The phone blinked to life. I called 911. When asked where we were, in trying to reply I choked off into a screeching run of coughs. I remembered the plastic bottle I'd taken from the daypack. Swallowing water hurt. My throat seemed scarcely open. I gave the water to Karen. I told the 911 operator where we were as best as I could guess.

She said, "How far off the main trail?"

"Less than a hundred feet."

"Hold your position. Cal Fire will call you in a few minutes. Don't call anybody. Save the battery."

Two hours and a phone check-in later, three souls stepped through hovering smoke. They had on yellow helmets with lights that wavered at every step. They wore yellow non-flammable overalls and yellow vests of the same material. They breathed through respirators. One carried a double bladed axe. All three hauled backpacks. Two men and a woman.

Karen and I called to them. They headed toward the melted snow and granite boulder we'd used as cover. At reaching the shallow pool, they kicked water onto the surrounding grit, which still had red spots, burning embers.

We were given canteens and told to drink slowly, and to take breaths between swallows.

"Ladies first," the woman said. "Over here."

Karen stepped through the shallow water. One of the guys emptied his pack. Out came stretchy fireproof booties to go over shoes, coveralls and a vest like he wore. Next was an N95 mask. Last, a yellow hard hat.

The woman said, "Next."

I said, "Two other cars were by where we parked. We're the brown Subaru. Is everyone accounted for?"

"Only your car and a silver Accord are there now. No knowledge of passengers. Don't talk about it. Save your strength."

As they finished with me, the woman said, "Are you two okay to walk?"

Karen and I coughed in unison while saying yes.

The woman said, "Henry will lead. We'll take an arm."

We and our escorts followed Henry, who carried the long axe. His head went up and down, checking for pockets of fire and not losing the trail. The woman said something into a phone about coming down with two survivors. Slow going for an hour and a half. We passed a crew raking debris. Waves were exchanged.

Shortly after that we approached a group of people examining the ground, some in uniform, others in civilian clothes. Two firefighters herded us around them in a wide half-circle. We stopped. Karen and I were stripped of gear and masks. The two men stuffed their bags.

Everything looked hazy.

The woman said, "They got to join mop up. We have another mile. Don't be shy about asking for help."

That mile seemed like two. Finally, I saw my brown Subaru, the Honda Accord, half a dozen large red vehicles and a white ambulance. Karen and I steadied each other. The woman followed close behind, I assumed ready to catch either of us if falling.

She helped us into the back of the ambulance, then waved overhead and walked in the direction of the fire.

The ambulance had one gurney. I said Karen should have it. The nurse said I looked worse off; I limped from bouncing my back down the granite boulder. I shook my head no.

The nurse said, "Like I told you, you need to be flat."

"I won't take it. Period. She's the one who saved us."

Karen was strapped onto the gurney.

I hobbled to a chair. When sitting, my knees buckled. The nurse grabbed my shoulders to keep me from spilling out of the chair. He clicked a seatbelt around my waist. I scarcely saw ahead. A siren came to life. It sounded far away.

Twenty

Morning light seeped through curtains. I gazed around a hospital room. Everything appeared vague. Each item merged with what was next to it. Outside the room, people walked by speaking in subdued voices. My throat hurt. Moving my torso brought jolts of pain down my spine.

Karen said, "I'm supposed to buzz them when you wake up. They'll shine a flashlight in your eyes, do a diagnostic."

"My engine's more in need of a tune-up."

"Mine's out of gas. They gave us something to knock us out last night, but it doesn't seem like I should feel this weak."

A Dr. Boucher came in. Short, stocky, bald headed, he had inquisitive eyes that darted here and there as he checked on me. I was fine except the raw lips, knotted back and butt muscles, and general fatigue. Dr. Boucher said Karen and I would be there another night. He'd reevaluate in the morning. I asked the nurse if I could have my phone. From it I learned the fire, dubbed Kamen II, was burning mostly into the Kamen Fire scar. It threatened few structures. I turned off the phone, closed my eyes, tried and failed to sleep.

We consumed a limp hospital breakfast. Karen fell asleep. Each minute passed sluggishly. Everything seemed deficient of color. I finally sank into sleep, and dreamed I was in a smoke-filled cave, trying to find a way out, arriving at one dead end after another.

Our nurse woke me, saying, "A Mr. Lewis from Placerville is here to see you both."

As soon as she saw Karen and I were awake, the nurse left the room.

Tom Lewis: about sixty, square jawed, heavyset, gray haired, bifocals. He sat between the ends of our beds. He said he was with Cal Fire.

"I investigate possible arson cases. I'm going to need statements from you. We'll do them separately. Karen, I'm told you're in better condition to be moved." Lewis altered his posture; he barely fit in the visitor's chair. "We'll go to a private room for an interview. If you become too tired to answer questions, we can continue this afternoon."

Karen said, "We just went for a hike."

Lewis said, "I'll get a wheelchair."

An attendant wheeled Karen off. I checked my phone again for information about the fire. Nothing new. Half an hour later, Lewis returned without Karen. He showed his I.D. and read me my rights. You know, I could request the presence of an attorney and anything I said could be used against me in court. Lewis asked me to sign a form declaring I consented to him recording our interview, and eyed my bad hand as I scribbled my name with his pen.

I reported everything that happened on the hike. Lewis asked a few questions. When he finished, he asked if there was anything I'd like to add. I told him about Brett's death, being harassed by the guy in a yellow windbreaker, and the fires that leveled Brett's chalet and garage a day later.

"You can get more details from a sergeant with South Tahoe police. His name's Jim Stevens."

Lewis had been listening with his head down, his iPhone doing the recording work. He looked up. "Jim Stevens? Known him for years."

After a lunch blander than breakfast, my head was clear and, besides the jolts of pain in my back, the world returned to normal. By three o'clock I was impatient being cooped up. Getting out of bed caused pain, but taking stiff steps to the bathroom helped loosen muscles. I was returning to bed when Stevens entered the room. At seeing Karen, he removed his patrolman's cap.

Stevens introduced himself. Karen introduced herself. She was treated to one of the sergeant's mini nods.

Karen, her voice still raw, said, "Were the people in a Honda, parked by us—were they found?"

"Two high school kids from Vacaville out for a hike. They'd taken the south slope trail. When they saw the fire, they ran down to the Carson River. CHP picked them up."

I said, "Arson?"

Stevens ran a hand into the gray buzz-cut and cowlick. "It was definitely set for a reason."

Karen rasped, "Meaning us?"

Stevens said, "More likely than not. Unfortunately, I've got more bad news. He got another one."

I said, "But your people contacted all the skiers. Made it clear not to open anything."

"He changed methods. You remember Mindy Morris, from the event?"

"Of course."

"Yesterday morning, she goes to her car. In Cold Springs, down by Mammoth. She drives off. A mile later Morris leaves the road and hits a tree. Turns out cyanide had been worked into the heater vents. It blew right in her face. A man driving behind her says he saw her let go of the steering wheel and grab her throat."

Karen said, "Oh my god."

Stevens said, "We did get a break, so to speak. Because of what happened to Brett and Fingler, local police were keeping tabs on Morris's movements. They were on scene fast and kept people away from the vehicle until a hazmat crew arrived."

Karen's forehead hatched its signature frown, "You guys have to stop this."

Stevens turned to her. "It's not 'you guys.' It's law enforcement. Four counties are involved now. I'm here to ask if either of you saw or heard anything yesterday, anything at all, that seemed out of place."

We both said nothing other than the fire.

Stevens tapped his patrolman's cap against his stomach. He turned away from me, toward Karen. "The result of Jeff's freelancing in the Boyd case will be about a thousand acres of burned national forest. Who knows how much money to put it out."

Two more things to feel guilty about.

Karen said, "We just went for a hike. Blame the killer, not us."

Stevens replaced his cap. "Thank you for your cooperation. If you remember anything that may help our investigation, you know how to contact me."

Stevens left.

The afternoon seemed endless. Dinner made it a string of three meals reminiscent of wet cardboard. Karen got up and walked around some, came back to bed.

Elise swept into the room.

"You *dears*," she said. "I'm so sorry. So very sorry."

Elise found a side table to place a glass vase with a rainbow of flowers in it. She remained standing. "Karen, how can you look this good after that ordeal yesterday?"

"You might want to visit an ophthalmologist."

Elise stepped between the two beds. She reached out with both arms; Elise had a remarkable wingspan. Without thinking I gave her my hand and I imagine Karen's hand went to Elise's in the same way.

Elise said, "How can I help?" She looked to Karen. "I've got the best dermatologist ever. He's in Santa Monica. You're to use him, on me. I do see a little damage."

Karen said, "Elise, please calm down. We're fine."

Elise let go of our hands, pirouetted a full circle, sighed, and sat. "My neighbor called. From Brett's gathering? She saw it online. I just had to come."

"Thanks for coming," I said.

It quickly became apparent Elise had little to say. During our times together we'd developed a quiet mutual tenderness, but other than Brett, we had nothing in common. The three of us made small talk for a few minutes, then Elise said she should let us rest.

"Call me if you need anything. Any, single, thing."

Twenty-one

We were discharged the next day. Judy Roiland, one of Karen's new colleagues, offered to drive us home during her lunch break. Once there, Karen drove us to where we'd parked on Saturday. The Honda Accord was gone. A CHP car had replaced it. The fire scar was seen from the road, beginning about a mile up. Kamen II's smoke was on the far side of Freedom Peak, not visible, drifting eastward. I waved to the officer, pointed to my car. He nodded and returned to tapping on some kind of tablet. I followed Karen to Fallen Leaf Lake. Entering The Lodge, the fireplace smell greeted us. It was a welcome reminder that the rambling cabin was becoming our home. I tore off bits of French bread and lined them along the back porch railing. Blue jays ate and squawked and jumped about.

After a meal that seemed grand compared to the hospital food, Karen and I conked out for a couple of hours. Later, we walked a bit along Cathedral Road.

Days were becoming shorter. With mountains to the west, evening fell before six. The quiet was soothing. Shortly after dark: rapping on the back door. I snatched the red switchblade off the coffee table.

I said, "Back bedroom. Keep the light off."

Karen hastily left the room. I moved to behind the corner at the hallway and snapped open the six-inch blade. I reached high with the knife, ready to slash downward. I'd practiced my grip with the thumb and forefinger of my better coordinated half hand.

A voice came through the door. "Jeff? Karen? Where are you folks?"

I leaped into the room, thrusting the red-handled knife forward. Jim Stevens and another man stood under the back porch light. I opened the door but stepped back and kept the knife out.

Stevens, in uniform, unsnapped his holster.

The man with him, Stevens' six feet but thicker, looked to Stevens. His face did not show fear. His manner made clear he was the senior officer. He said, "You warned me he can be thorny." The man stepped inside and offered his right hand. "Ted Post. South Tahoe PD."

Stevens said, "Chief of police."

Stevens came inside, shut the door. I closed the knife, put it in my left palm and shook hands with Post. "After what happened, we're jumpy."

Post said, "I'd be jumpy, too."

"I didn't hear a car. You usually hear cars from far away out here."

Stevens said, "We'll explain."

He re-snapped his holster. Post seemed amused.

I called behind me. "No worries. We have visitors."

We sat in front of the fireplace. Short yellow flames licked wood.

Karen glided out. Her face still showed red marks from fleeing the fire. Stevens introduced her to Chief Post. Karen sat next to me on the green couch.

Post, casually dressed, including dark running shoes, told us he had established a stakeout at number eleven Cathedral Road. The Lodge was number fourteen, on the other side of the street. The stakeout was predicated on the arson fire that chased us; the arson fire that leveled Brett's chalet and garage; other information

Stevens had provided Post over the previous few weeks.

"Jim's friends with the Knox family, owners of eleven. They gave us permission to go ahead. There's a decent sight line to here. I initiated everything last night in case our suspect decided to play fire bug again."

Karen and I looked at each other. We'd just settled down after Saturday's escape.

I said, "You don't have to ask us about any of this?"

He shook his broad head. Post's eyes were soft. They expressed genuine kindness. "It's my job to keep people safe. What Jim's told me about the fires and the man in question means you require protection. And to be honest, you're the best bait we have. The best bait to catch a likely perpetrator of three murders."

"Somehow I don't feel special."

Karen patted my thigh. "Face it, Jeff. You're a target."

Post said, "I'd categorize it more as a potential target."

"Categorize it however you want," Karen said. "I'll tell you what I want. I want this person caught before he does any more damage."

Post said, "Absolutely."

Stevens said, "We're all on the same basic page."

I said, "Tell me more about this basic page."

Post gestured to Stevens.

Stevens folded his hands together. "We have zero solid leads. A few grainy pictures of him at a restaurant where he did nothing wrong. The license plate of a vehicle rented to someone using fake I.D. No fingerprints. You know all this. The point is, he has a pattern of following a strike with a return trip. Remember I told you about Mindy Morris getting poisoned?"

"Of course."

"We got word this morning a fire broke out in the tow yard where her car got shipped and cordoned off."

Post said, "This guy moves nonstop. We have to be ready."

I said, "What about Karen?"

"We've arranged for her to stay with a female officer," Post said. "It's safer than staying at a motel."

"If you think I'm leaving Jeff, you can forget it."

Post ran a hand back over thick brown hair. "I can't force you. I'd like to convince you of what's in your best interest. He's killed three, made an attempt on Jim's life. Will you at least consider it?"

"I'm not sure," Karen said.

Post said, "Another possibility is, if Jeff doesn't feel safe here, you both move in with the officer. We'd leave your cars, make it look like you're in residence. Think things over. For the sake of the investigation, you should decide by tomorrow. We want to stay ahead of any future developments."

Post stood. He took out his wallet and extracted two business cards. He handed one to Karen, the other to me. "On the back, the top number is the command phone for the stakeout. You can call twenty-four seven. It doesn't matter if it turns out to be a chipmunk. Any fear, you call. The second number is my private cell. One final thing. No matter what, don't go to eleven. Our suspect may be watching at any time. In fact, we walked here in a roundabout way Jim knew. That's why you didn't hear a vehicle."

Stevens looked at me. "You saved my life. I intend to do the same for you."

Post said, "If you call the team, or they call you, the first words spoken are Sky Lake. That makes it clear it's not a setup. Same thing in any call to or from me. First words are Sky Lake."

A little more handshaking, and they were off into the night. Karen and I stood with arms around each other. I looked up to the odd red wood bird chandelier. For the first time, I noticed the lightbulb in its mouth burned brighter than the others. I perused the room, much as my mother had for the first time. The Lodge was a wonderful place to live.

The Lodge was a place we could easily be ambushed.

Karen said, "What do you think?"

"I'm still wondering how he knew it was my car, parked at the trailhead."

"Don't you think it was from leaving it at Elise's overnight?"

"I don't know. It doesn't matter. Will you consider going along with the police on this?"

Karen said, "They're going to watch nonstop. Isn't that enough?"

"I can't even guess."

Karen insisted on going to work the next day. I walked her to her car. The orange Volvo drove off. I took a stroll along Cathedral Road, working out stiffness in my back. I passed house number eleven. It appeared no one was there.

I drove to the post office in South Lake Tahoe. Neither Karen nor I had opened our P.O. box in a week, which was not unusual because we received little mail. I removed a thick wad of paper. Went to a recycling bin and flipped through ads and envelopes, discarding one thing after another, until an envelope had *Safe To Open* typed and Scotch taped in place of a return address. Our P.O. box number was also typed and taped to the envelope. I jogged to my car, set the envelope on its roof, opened the back door and took out my black doctor's bag. Inside were disinfectant wipes; I used a few on my hands. I slipped on blue medical exam gloves, took two wipes and sealed the envelope in a Ziploc bag. I set the Ziploc bag on the backseat and wiped down the clasp of the doctor's bag.

I called Chief Post. "Sky Lake." I told him about the envelope and putting it in a plastic bag.

"I'll tell Froug. You've met her, right, that time with Jim?"

"Yes."

"She'll be at the entrance. Nobody else touches that envelope."

In a hazmat suit, Alicia Froug waited outside the glass police department entrance doors. I'd put on a fresh set of gloves before driving; I transferred the Ziploc bag to her gloved hands.

Froug said, "Wait in the staff room. Your gloves go on the floor, in a corner. Wash up to your elbows. Don't touch your face. Follow me."

In the less-than-charming staff room, I fidgeted on my phone. Because it mostly burned in the Kamen fire scar, Kamen II was already sixty percent contained. I looked around the room of metal chairs, metal tables, empty walls. Both windows were closed. On my phone I found and recorded water skier La Porte's home and business addresses, his phone number and the email address of his business.

Chief Post entered the room. He wore a blue uniform with a metal five-star badge pinned at the heart. No gun. He carried an envelope and a piece of typing paper folded into thirds. He set them in front of me.

Post walked around the table, and sat. Calm as a bird watcher, he said, "One hundred percent clean. Froug knows her stuff. Take a look."

I hesitated. Post licked a finger, touched the letter, then rubbed the finger across his lips. "See?"

I unfolded the sheet of paper. Typed across its center: Jeff Taylor #14 Cathedral Road car license RQU256

I said, "He's not exactly subtle."

"Notice the envelope postmark?"

"No."

"It's postmarked last Friday, and stamped Fresno. This guy

never stops moving. Twenty-four hours later he's up north again, lighting a forest on fire. You said he seemed high on something, in the restaurant. Maybe he's a meth head."

"He's a something head. It oozes out of him."

Post said, "I can't give these to you, but tell your wife about it. That might inform her thinking about staying at the cabin."

I said I'd tell her.

Post said, "Let this inform your thinking, too. Like I said, we can leave both cars in the carport, get you rentals. Install timers on lamps to make it look like people are inside when it's dark. It's not perfect, but it's worth a shot."

At home late that afternoon, I told Karen about the one-page note with my name and address typed on it.

She said, "These past few days feel more like a few weeks."

We'd finished dinner but had not taken dishes away. Outside, moonlight explored the surface of Fallen Leaf Lake. It was seen in chunks between tree trunks. Its milkiness showed as ripples in the water.

I said, "You came back to a mess. I'm sorry."

Karen shrugged. It came with a frown.

A gunshot sounded as a bullet splintered a windowpane. One of the windows that looked onto the back porch and down to the lake. Glass clattered across the dining table and wood floor.

We crawled under the table. I took out my phone and hit the stakeout command number.

A man answered: "Sky Lake. Heard it. On our way. Keep out of sight."

Insistent knocking rattled the front door. A male voice boomed, "Sky Lake! Open up."

I duck-walked to the door. It unlocked as I turned the handle and swung it open. A man about thirty, in street clothes, carrying a walkie-talkie, stepped inside and shut the door behind him.

He said, "Where's your wife?"

I pointed to the dining table. The man spoke into the walkie-talkie. "Subjects accounted for. Loanne, go west. Bob, east."

I rejoined Karen under the table. A hushing whistle passed overhead as breeze made its way through the window hole.

I noted the man from cabin number eleven was armed. He motioned for Karen and me to stay under the table. He looked at the glass fragments on the floor, then sat clear of them.

"We stay still. We listen."

We listened. The only sound was the hushing wind coming through the shattered window. Karen and I remained hunched under the dining table. My heart pounded hard nonstop. Finally, a knock on the front door.

Coming through the officer's walkie-talkie: "Sky Lake. It's me."

The officer opened the door for Chief Post.

Post said, "Check on Kuller and Smith. If one is on a trail with possibilities, you follow. Otherwise, call 'em back. I'll go over from here to debrief."

"Yes, sir."

The officer left through the front door.

Post said, "May I?" He pointed to one of the wicker chairs, and sat.

Karen and I sat on the green couch.

Post said, "From the top."

There wasn't much to tell.

Post stood. "If nothing else, you should be safe here. Our cover's blown. For now, I'll keep the stake active. Starting in the morning, when either of you plan to leave, call fifteen minutes before. Give your destination. We'll watch for a tail." Post shook hands with Karen, shook hands with me. "Goodnight."

Post left through the front door. He checked from outside to make sure it locked.

Twenty-two

Morning. Karen called the stakeout and said she'd be driving to Barton Memorial in fifteen minutes.

An email from Margaret Field expressed concern regarding Karen and me, and the fire. The newspapers had reported us as survivors. The two boys from Vacaville weren't named because they were minors. No mention of Brett Boyd's death, the burned chalet and garage, or anything other than Kamen II had been declared arson. I figured that was good for all parties, especially me. Dr. Field wrote we should get together soon, with Ron Hart, for dinner with spouses at her and her husband's condo in Tahoe Keys.

The message ended with: Hired.

Elation. I replied with thanks, and asked what day was best for her. I heard a car approach on Cathedral Road. I peered through the glass upper half of the front door. A white South Lake Tahoe police cruiser, in full view of anyone watching, went onto the short driveway before the car port. It reversed a partial circle, lurched ahead over fallen pine needles, and parked. Chief Post got out. Head down, both hands went to the car roof.

I made a request of the gods that Post wasn't there because of something involving Karen.

Post walked to the front door. I opened it. Post looked like he hadn't slept. He did not offer to shake hands. He ambled into the living room and sat on a wicker chair.

"Jim's dead. The suspect, too."

I stood near the center of the huge room. Above me loomed the hideous red wood bird chandelier. I looked away from it and out the square windows showing the back porch railing and chunks of the dark lake. I'd taped a piece of cardboard over the shattered window. The broken window and piece of taped cardboard no longer seemed symbols of a threat. They seemed trivial.

My words came in a halting, tentative whisper. "What, happened?"

I sat across from the chief. His face was gray, and sadder than I would've imagined he'd ever be. His gentle nature was born twinned with an amiable countenance, but Stevens' death had floored him.

Post said, "Last night, Jim heard dispatch report gunfire in the Fallen Leaf area. He always took a patrol car home. Lived with dispatch on inside. Jim tells dispatch he knows a trail from Fallen Leaf Campground to here. Says that's a way to get from here to a car and back on the highway without raising suspicion."

Chief Post swallowed. He seemed dry. His gaze went to the floor. "Jim heads out. He's got the siren going. They hear it at dispatch. He goes in Fallen Leaf Road. Campground's maybe half a mile."

"Any car speeding out is our guy."

Post nodded. "Jim's hauling ass. No streetlights, no buildings. Last thing he says is, 'Around a turn at me.'"

Post's face seemed drained of blood. "Head on with an SUV. Both drivers casualties. Jim and the suspect. No passengers in the SUV."

I couldn't stay still. I walked a circle. My steps were clumsy. "This shouldn't happen. He's too young for this to happen."

My helpless words seemed to prompt Post back into his role as leader. He pushed on his knees and stood.

"I'd like you to identify the other driver. You're the only

individual who has seen the other party multiple times, in multiple arenas."

"Why are you sure it's him?"

"I'm not at liberty to disclose evidence until after you identify the body." Post stepped toward the door. "Follow me in." He stopped. As if talking to himself, Post said, "When I was growing up, on weekends Jim would come to the high school and play soccer with the big kids. He was always around. He was like a younger brother."

I followed the police car to South Lake Tahoe. As when driving to the odd gathering for Brett, the towering trees lining Highway 89 took on the quality of mourners. I'd lived at Fallen Leaf Lake for a month. Two people connected to me were dead, Brett and Stevens. I wasn't to blame. I felt guilty. I told myself to not feel guilty. I wasn't guilty but wasn't innocent, either.

At the South Lake Tahoe Police Department, those brown rock walls, pine trees lining the edges of the parking lot, I got out of the Subaru and joined Post at the glass doors. We went inside. There was no showing I.D. or slowing through the metal detector. Everyone in the building exhibited knowledge of Chief Post's pain, and their own. The anguish that owned their faces stung me.

We passed the office where Stevens had worked. Post exited at the end of the hall and led me to a back parking lot for department employees. On the other side of the lot we entered the coroner's office. If the halls and rooms in the main building could be called muted, the inside of the coroner's office was an electrified white. Every inch of the large space shined brightly under banks of high-powered bulbs resting in metal cages. A floor of white linoleum. White walls. The temperature was refrigerator cold. The coroner himself wore a white lab coat, dark slacks and squeaky white nurse's shoes. Fiftyish, overweight, freckled, the man rubbed his hands together as if about to dig into a warm meal.

Post said, "Marty. How's things?"

Marty took out a handkerchief, blew his nose on it, viewed the result. "If it weren't for this damn cold, which has taken up residence, I'd say life is pretty good. Which one?" Marty walked to a wall with rectangles showing, wide as coffins though half as tall.

Post said, "Not Jim."

Marty went to a pair of metal handles. He pulled, triggering a noise like the metal wheels of a skateboard rolling across a sidewalk. Out emerged a sheet-covered dead person. He or she was on plank-like steel. Light bounced off the steel like sunlight bounces off the fender of a car. The coroner walked away, to a body he was attending to.

I said, "What's his name?"

"After you identify. We don't want to influence." Post gestured to the white sheet. "He's mangled. Not so bad you won't recognize him."

I took a breath, lifted the sheet, looked. My chest felt like firecrackers exploded in it. My gasp was that of a person struggling to breathe. I dropped the sheet, stepped backwards, bent at the knees and put both hands on the white floor to avoid collapsing.

Post steadied me. "Seeing a corpse for the first time, lots of people react like this. Don't worry about it."

"It's not him."

"We have evidence. The vehicle was another rental. A six-month lease with an early return option. In it was a handgun, recently fired. I guarantee you it'll match any bullet we recover at your place." Post gestured toward the lump of white sheet. "Would you take another look?"

"His name's David Gummer."

"From Reno. He's got a record of violence against men who end up with his ex girlfriends. He used to be tight with Brett Boyd's widow. According to Jim, you've been keeping her company. There were photographs of Elise Jansen in the vehicle. In a briefcase were newspaper articles about Brett printed from online sources. Also about you and your wife, regarding Kamen II. It was like his trophy case. We're gaining info by the hour."

A stomach knot held me in a nauseating grip. "It's my fault. Both of them are my fault."

Post said, "You don't look okay. And you're not making sense."

"Can we get out of here?"

"Come on. Let's get you calmed down."

Post helped me up. I kept my hands out in front as we walked because I didn't see well. Post opened the back door to the police department. He let me enter first, taking my elbow like you would a very old person whose balance was off.

In the drab staff room, over cups of water, I told Chief Post about going to Reno to see Gummer, thinking him a potential suspect in Brett's murder. I told him Gummer made crude sexual remarks about Elise, that I struck him twice and he just took it. I said he showed up sloppy drunk that night at Elise's, and begged her to get back together. I told Post Gummer passed out. That when I slapped him awake he pissed his pants, thus humiliating himself in front of Elise. I said I checked him into a motel, took his car so he couldn't drive while blitzed.

I recounted Gummer's threat to get back at me when I dropped him off outside the motel room.

Like when my hand got chopped, everything closed in on me, squeezed me so I felt small, in a small room. My racing thoughts all led to the same truth: My obsession with finding Brett's killer was the reason Jim Stevens and David Gummer were dead.

Post stood. He, too, was unsteady. He walked to the other side of the staff room. His uniformed back to me, his voice low though not soft, Post said, "I asked you to stay here, while I get someone to take a statement. You didn't answer. Does this mean you refuse?"

"I don't remember hearing it. Of course I'll make a statement."

Post turned around. He growled, "Stay here. You'll give Officer Phillips your statement, then you go out the back door. I don't want my people even seeing you. Not after what you just told me." A vein in Post's neck visibly throbbed. "You repeat this to no one but Officer Phillips. You hear me? Jim was killed trying to save you after you reported a gunshot. That's all we say. We keep the stakeout. Your man in the yellow windbreaker probably doesn't know about it. I want to continue to use you for bait. I guarantee you this guy's not done killing people."

I walked to the closed window that allowed yellowish light into the room. Outside were parked cars, pine trees. Nothing new. Yet the Chief's words—*this guy's not done killing people*—turned my need to catch the sicko from an obsession into desperation.

"I owe it to Jim Stevens to stay at the house."

"You're goddamn right you do."

Chief Post left the room.

Twenty-three

I stopped at Raley's Market and, without much noticing what I selected, stocked up, four bags of groceries. A shroud of self doubt enveloped me. Knowing my life had taken another sudden crash kept my stomach knotted.

Parked just past the carport, a South Lake Tahoe police car. An officer got out as I turned into the open-ended carport. He'd come to search for the bullet of the night before. He gave me his name; I didn't catch it. I showed him the cardboard covering the hole, then unloaded groceries. All this happened in a dense fog. The officer asked for a ladder. He dug a bullet out of the ceiling a few feet from the front door. I signed a form, handed it back to the officer, and he left.

I tried to remember if the policeman had said anything about the bullet he recovered. Or anything else. I ordered myself to sit down. To sit and try to think straight. My phone jingled. Elise. I didn't want to answer. I had to answer.

"Hello."

Elise said, "I can't believe it. I *can't*. David and Jim Stevens, gone? The police chief came by to ask questions."

"It's a huge shock." I instantly felt foolish. "What a thoughtless understatement."

"Are we partly to blame? For sending David into the night like that?"

"You're not. I am."

"What are you talking about?"

"I went to his office in Reno. To ask about Brett. To be sure he didn't do it."

"When?"

"I roughed him up in the morning, before he later went to your place. I knocked him down. He just took it. At your place he was humiliated right in front of you. That led to him wanting revenge. Led to a gunshot through the window last night."

"Why hit David?"

"He said sexual things about you that were inexcusable. I lost my head."

Voice cracking, Elise said, "He always had a big mouth. You shouldn't have taken him seriously."

"I know that now."

Elise said, "I'm hella scared. The chief says he's putting a watch on my house. I don't want to live like this."

"I understand."

"You always do. That's why I'm calling. I need a ride. I'm afraid to get in an Uber or a taxi with a stranger, because of what the chief told me. If you could come by, I'll be forever grateful. I know I'll be safe with you till I'm gone."

"Gone?"

"Come by. We'll talk about it then."

Three suitcases and a carry-on bag sat in the entry hall at Elise's sprawling wood house. Rather than stretch out on the shiny brown leather couch, she sat adjacent to me in one of the russet chairs.

"Before I forget, the basketball DVDs are in that bag on the table."

"Did you ever watch them?"

"Over and over. I finally stole 'em and hid them here, so he'd quit making me watch with him. I convinced Brett he mislaid them during a binge."

I glanced at the suitcases. "What's going on?"

"After the police chief scared the crap out of me, I called Annabee. Like I always do when I'm stuck. She invited me to come down. Annabee owns this little court south of Wilshire, in Beverly Hills. Her place is two floors. Attached to it are four one bedroom apartments. She keeps one empty for visiting mods. She offered it."

"Obviously," I said, "you accepted."

A wave of relief came over me.

"It's more than that. I'm moving back to Los Angeles. I'll get a lot more gigs." Elise swung her long hair. "Annabee has three newbies, eighteen, eighteen, and twenty. She wants me to school them. Not just how to present, but how to survive in that batshit scene."

I looked at the world Elise had created, the paintings, the sculptures, bookshelves, impeccable furnishings. "You said you were done with all that."

"It's what I know. I'm thirty-one years old, and don't want to spend my life sitting on my ass drinking every day."

"What about all this?"

"Annabee's sending up her assistant. She'll take care of renting the house. Ship the furnishings to storage. She'll manage everything except the insurances. Annabee's lawyer was already on it with the insurance companies." Elise seemed anxious. "Will you stay with me, until I go?"

"I'll stay till you board."

"Say goodbye to Karen for me."

"Of course."

Elise said, "I called Mixx. You two have a night on my credit card."

186

She couldn't hold back. She wept, this time not trying to avoid me seeing it. Leaving South Lake Tahoe, leaving behind those charred piles, Brett's ashes in Sky Lake: it marked the end of Elise and Brett.

"Isn't this kind of fast?"

"I'm sick of thinking I might get killed. I trust Annabee's advice. I don't have any life here without Brett." Elise placed fingertips together, as if in prayer. "Will you and Karen have gin gimlets? Promise me you will."

Twenty-four

At the airport I observed the polite, public relations side of Elise, certainly part of what Annabee wanted Elise to transfer to her newly signed models. Elise shook hands with two women who approached her separately. Next, she posed for photos, taken by me, with a thirty-something couple who were also flying to Los Angeles. Elise introduced me by name and as South Lake Tahoe's newest doctor.

Elise's plane took off. Looking south by southeast, no smoke marred the horizon. Kamen Fire II was essentially extinguished. One good development amidst no developments regarding Brett's murder.

I went home and for distraction popped a DVD into the player beneath a TV in one of the extra downstairs bedrooms. The DVDs were two for each of three AAU seasons, a full game, and highlights from others that year. Brett's parents did the camera work, edited the material and gave copies to everyone on the team. To my surprise it was not painful to watch a younger me run up and down basketball courts.

Karen came home. She held me tight. She led me to the couch. We kicked off our shoes and stretched out together.

Karen said, "I can tell you know what happened."

I nodded. I didn't offer what I knew. "How did you hear?"

"It's all anyone talks about. People are taking it hard. Gummer has become the local villain. I don't blame anyone for feeling that way. I mean, he shot our window because he thinks you're seeing Elise? And Stevens was coming to our aid? That's the rumor. Can things get any worse?"

"Let's not think about things getting worse."

Karen didn't know about my cheap shot strikes at Gummer in his office, or Gummer's humiliation at Elise's. I was the region's villain, not David Gummer.

My mind drifted in a kind of Jell-O-like space where nothing was stable. Or quite real.

Karen said, "What's that?"

She'd seen a painting, leaning against a wall below one of the front windows of The Lodge's great room. It was a landscape of hills in various shades of green, with subtle gold woven into the ridges. In the foreground were yellow and blue shapes suggestive of a village.

"Elise gave it to us. After being interviewed by Chief Post this morning, she's scared she might be the next victim. She took a plane to L.A. I drove her to the airport."

"Elise. Everywhere Elise. She's another person I know of who needs to find a job."

"She did. Or I should say a job found her."

"I don't mean two days parading on a runway. I mean a real job."

"Like I said, she did. Elise is scared half to death. Plus she realizes there's no life for her in Tahoe without Brett. She called her agent, Annabee Flowers. Remember hearing about her?"

"Who could forget her slapping her card into Elise's hand and walking away?"

I explained the arrangement Elise had made with Annabee. That I'd agreed to drive Elise to the airport because she was afraid to get in a car with a driver she didn't know. "When we were about to head out, she insisted I take the painting for us to remember her by."

Karen said, "I get why Elise left. I'm tired of worrying Brett's killer is going to show up. I'm tired of worrying what I might come home to, with you here alone all day."

That night, I brooded rather than slept.

The next morning, a front-page article in the *Tahoe Daily Tribune* announced a community gathering in honor of Sergeant Jim Stevens. Saturday, eleven o'clock, at Sky Lake. The article mentioned that Stevens' first job was working summers there as a teenager, and he'd kept ties to the summer families ever since. It went on to note that with no parking areas at the lake, private cars wouldn't be allowed. Five school buses would head out from South Lake Tahoe High School at ten-thirty. After speakers, a community lunch would be served, courtesy of local restaurants. On the list of donors was Antonio's Restaurant.

The article continued on page two. I didn't read the rest of the article because directly across from it, on page three, was the newspaper's daily Out & About photograph. These were sent in by readers showing average citizens and sometimes celebrities in the Tahoe area. Below the photo was a short paragraph giving the who, where and when the picture was taken. That morning's who was three-time *Vogue* cover model Elise Jansen clutching my arm while waiting in line at the airport. I was identified as "Jeff Taylor, SLT's newest doctor."

When Karen came home I asked if she'd seen the photograph in the paper, and if so, did it upset her.

"Of course it upsets me. You think it's fun, knowing people are talking behind your back? But we have more important things to deal with. I thought about it all day. We should take the chief's offer, stay with police until things are safe. It's dumb to sit here waiting for something awful to happen."

"You can go. I can't."

"Why not?"

"I gave Chief Post my word. I owe it to Stevens."

"You don't owe him anything. He's gone. Killed in the line of duty."

"I'm the best bait to catch this guy. I gave my word."

Karen walked across the expansive room, to the kitchen area. She opened the refrigerator door, then shut it hard. Its contents rattled. She called across the big house. "One last time. Can I tell the chief we're going, or are you staying?"

I joined Karen in the kitchen. I reached to put an arm around her. She stepped back.

I said, "I owe it to Stevens to help catch this guy."

"You're a goddamn stubborn mule."

Karen packed. She said discussing things would only lead to a fight, and we didn't have the luxury of going down that road right then. A goodbye kiss at her car, and Karen disappeared into darkness, taillights vanishing around the first curve.

Twenty-five

While sixty-three streams feed the blue miracle called Lake Tahoe, there is only one outlet, the Truckee River at Tahoe City. I drove from the south end of the lake to roughly its north end, crossed the Truckee River and curled north-east along the lake toward Nevada. I found La Porte Skis in a large metal shed-like structure. A dock and speedboats were forty feet from an entrance that was an aluminum garage door, wide open. I entered.

A five-time world slalom champion, Bob La Porte had racked up victories at major water ski tournaments into his forties. He'd moved onto designing and crafting—meaning with his own hands—slalom skis. People came from all over the globe to have La Porte create a custom ski for them.

Eyes adjusting after an hour of uninterrupted bold mountain sunlight, I approached a bear of a man who operated a blowtorch with the ease others utilize a dinner fork. About my six feet three, his shoulders were wide as a doorway. I half-shouted hello. La Porte extinguished a hissing, blue-tipped flame. He said, "Cable's back in the office."

La Porte pulled off heavy gloves, set them on a wood counter, and removed goggles. He took a rag from a back pocket and wiped his face while stepping across a cement floor. Various materials covered most of the area. Partially finished slender skis lined one rack; a smaller rack held a ski that seemed done. Painted across its Tahoe-blue topside, in thin black cursive: *For Steinbush by La Porte.*

He crossed the room. "It just cut out on me. I'm supposed to watch this show, to prep for interviewing the winners."

La Porte's hair was an equal mix of gray and a quiet brown. He took an opened plastic bottle of water off a different wood counter and downed a slug. The shop smelled of glue, the discharge of the flames, wood and sheets of fiberglass.

I said, "I'm not here about cable TV. I'm here about Brett Boyd."

La Porte stopped walking. He seemed to really notice me for the first time. "What about Brett? Even though we didn't get along, I had nothing against him. Are you with the police?"

"I'm an old friend of Brett's. My name's Jeff Taylor. I'm trying to get to the bottom of what happened to him."

We shook hands. A speedboat zipped by behind me. Its engine wailed, faded. La Porte gave my half hand a glance, no more. He emptied the plastic water bottle, left it on the wood counter. His green eyes were calm yet intense in a glassy sort of way.

He said, "Let's go to the office."

We sat, La Porte behind a desk, me on a folding chair with a ragged brown cushion that had white paint stains splattered across it. His chair was some kind of squeaky thing. Behind La Porte were two thumbtacked posters. One was of him skiing; a remarkable rooster tail of water vaulted behind him. The other was a close up of a La Porte water ski. A small electric fan slept on the desk, which was not big and not showy.

He said, "I'm sorry about what happened, but hell, I get a lot of packages from Fed Ex. Now they go directly to the sheriff's office. Every piece of mail does. Sometimes it takes days for them to bring it over. I have deadlines."

"If I can find the guy who ended Brett's life, you won't have that problem anymore. How do you remember him?"

"When he first came on the circuit, he was a talented eighteen-year-old. Tremendous balance. He needed to build leg power. People don't realize how much strain slalom puts on your legs."

"I read he was a star right away."

"Not really. He came into his own the third summer. He finished close behind me in the Masters, I think fourth in the Worlds. That winter, he beat me in Florida. After that it was either one of us, or Al Shepard, for the big ones. This went on for years, till he got hurt."

"Why didn't you get along with him?"

"Everybody treated Brett like a rock star. Even though I still won more tournaments," La Porte said, and motioned out toward his shop, "I was the blue collar, nuts and bolts guy. The wild man Boyd thing attracted more ink."

"I saw the article in *Sports Illustrated*."

La Porte said, "After a few years, I let go of the rivalry. Brett wouldn't. By then he was a big-time media presence. He married a supermodel. You know who I mean?"

"I know Elise."

"After he tore the hamstring, suddenly he's not a star. Pictures of him aren't all over the internet. He went downhill pretty fast. Then he just quit."

La Porte looked up, over my head, checking to see if somebody had entered the shop.

I said, "What I'm looking for are Brett's enemies."

"No way would one of the skiers kill him. Burn down his house? Not even close."

"I'm not thinking just water skiers. Anybody stick out, in a certain town, maybe a bar fight, a money situation? I know he had a history of money problems."

La Porte stood. "Look. I can't help you. And I should get back out there. I don't want to miss the cable guy."

We left the office. La Porte went to the wood counter, picked up the thick gloves and slapped them together. He fingered the goggles but didn't put them on. I took the hint.

"Let me leave you my number and email, in case something comes to mind."

La Porte found a pen and a tablet of yellow paper. I wrote down the information. We shook hands. I drove south along the spectacular lake.

At Fallen Leaf I took a long brisk walk along Cathedral Road, depending on the police to keep me safe. It felt good to have the stiffness from after the fire gone. I ate dinner, and downed a few beers while watching highlights of Team Far North outplaying city all-star teams. Beer and old times couldn't replace the empty feeling in The Lodge that came with Karen's absence.

My shot swished through the net without touching the rim. Brett made a basket. I passed to David Brown open down low; he dunked ferociously.

My phone woke me. Another number not in my contacts list. "Hello."

"Bob La Porte here. I've been thinking about Brett. The more I do, the more I realize if my career got trashed in my twenties, I probably wouldn't have dealt with it very good, either. It makes me take this more seriously."

"Good," I said, "because I'm not quitting until either I or the cops find his killer."

I pictured La Porte sitting at the scarred wood desk. He said, "There was a lot of drama with Brett. He attracted it. One time we were at this lake in Georgia. Two days before a tournament, everybody's taking practice runs. This guy about Brett's age corners him and demands Brett get him entered. He backs Brett up against a wall. He says something like, 'You're afraid I'll beat you. That's why you won't get me in.'"

I snatched a notebook and began writing.

"Brett explains only ranked skiers can compete. He tries to get the guy to calm down, go to the tournament office, but the guy's all over Brett. I thought Brett was getting payback for some of his showboating. I kind of liked it. The guy finally walks away talking to himself."

"Did he have a thick scar above his right eyebrow?"

"Not that I noticed."

"What did Brett say about it?"

"Said it was a jerk he hadn't seen in years, who just shows up one day and makes an impossible demand."

"What'd he look like?"

"Like he could make trouble. Solid. I don't know, brown hair, not long, not short. About six feet."

"You were in the south. Did he have an accent?"

"If he did, I don't remember it."

"Anything else you can think of? Did Brett say his name?"

"No. But a couple years later, we're at Imperial Lakes, down by the Mexican border. They got a freakin' great ski park. I hear Brett in a shouting match with a guy in the parking lot. Me and Mitch Wright—a skier—go check it out. It's the same dude as in Georgia. Arguing he should be in the tournament. Says he has documentation for his runs, but the officials won't let him in. Brett better fix it. Mitch shoves the dude about five times, till he finally leaves. Brett blew it off, like before. It was part of his cool guy style. That's all I can think of."

"Thanks. Anything else comes to mind, call or email any time."

I hung up. Interesting, but without distinguishing physical I.D., not much.

I went to the extra bedroom that served as a den and popped in another DVD. The second DVD game was against the San Jose Eagles, after our junior year. Of course the games Brett's parents burned onto DVDs were ones we came out on top. Next, I popped in the highlights disc for that year. Most of the highlights were long jump shots or great blocks. A sequence came on versus the Kern County Cougars. An opponent goes chest-to-chest with Brett. Brett dribbles, one-two-three. He looks off, then shoots a bounce pass between the defender's legs to a cutting Bob Koury who catches it, plants his feet and pops in a jump shot.

More impressive three-point shots. Then that defender again pressuring Brett as Brett dribbles and waves two fingers, calling one of our plays. With Brett's hand up, the defender jams a hand against Brett's sternum. No foul called. Brett dribbles and takes a long step right. The defender's left leg goes out to stay with Brett; Brett delivers another bounce pass between the defender's legs. It goes to Gary Patterson, who passes the ball to David Brown. Brown lays the ball against the glass backboard for an easy two points.

The defender dips his chin, swivels it to the right. He thrusts a finger at Brett and says something that can't be understood.

I backed up the disc, stopped it. The defender was on the slim side. The dipping chin and looking right: I watched it several times.

I popped in the third year highlights. Just one play involved the in-Brett's-face defender I'd watched earlier. This time he's on offense. He dribbles past half court, cuts right fast. Brett dives, body even with the floor. He slaps the ball to Tom Vercelli who hits a streaking Patterson for a dunk.

The view of the opposition player is from behind. He dips his chin and turns it rightward.

After a few more viewings, I recalled the player. Anyone assigned to defend Brett would be the opposition's best defender, but there would be other plays where Brett tricked him that didn't appear in the highlights. Maybe a lot of them.

In the morning I called Roberto. I still wondered about the dynamics of him and Whitmer, but my focus was Brett's murder. I asked Roberto if he could capture screen shots from a DVD, and combine them with the pictures obtained from Antonio's video system.

"I'll be slammed most of the day. Come after six. Make a list of the screen times for capture."

In his cave of an office, I looked for signs Roberto was nervous because I'd bumped into him after he'd dealt in drugs with Whitmer. There were none. And I was confident he had no knowledge of being followed to the cemetery. Roberto created two attachments that he emailed to me. I forwarded them, with a brief message, to La Porte's business email address.

I slipped my phone away. "What should I give you, for your time?"

Roberto said, "Catch the son of a bitch."

Night falling, my car rolled between trees on Cathedral Road. La Porte called.

"That's him in the basketball pictures. I'm sure of it. Younger, not as built. Still, that pissed-off face. The gestures. The pictures in the bar, I have no idea."

Twenty-six

Margaret Field emailed an invitation for Karen and me to join her, Ron Hart and their spouses for dinner, six o'clock Friday evening. She apologized for the late Wednesday invite, explaining she'd been dealing with an unexpected personnel shortage at Barton Memorial, where Margaret was on the board of directors. I could hardly reply Karen was in hiding. The newspapers had only mentioned me and Karen as survivors of the Kamen II fire. No connections involving me to the deaths of Stevens and Gummer. No connections to Brett.

I figured Chief Post had a strategy. He sure as hell wasn't going to share it with me.

I called Karen and told her about the dinner invite. To my great relief, she didn't hesitate.

She said, "How about if I meet you in the lot at the turn-in for Cathedral? I'll be there at five-forty-five."

My immediate task was to get the name of the player who'd tangled with Brett on the court. I found the website of the Kern County Cougars. A different coach than from my era was in charge. I emailed him, listed the years I'd faced his team and asked for contact information regarding the coach of those years. Current Coach Hopkins responded that while he couldn't give me the old coach's name and contact information, he'd pass mine onto him.

*   *   *

Karen's dusky orange Volvo didn't pull into the commuters' lot at five-forty-five on Friday. A burly tan pickup, rust at the fenders, swung in and halted behind where I waited. Karen emerged. She'd brushed her hair out of its ponytail. Her dress, which crossed her knees, was long sleeved and faint, modest in color.

I reached across and opened the door. Karen slid into the passenger seat. "Taylor," she said. She leaned over and kissed my cheek.

I said, "It's important you come tonight. I still don't officially have the position."

Karen said, "I needed to get out of that place. It's weird living with someone who keeps a gun on the kitchen table."

I pointed behind us. "Your protector?"

"They won't let me go anywhere alone. They say since he has your license plate, he probably has mine."

I turned on headlights and drove to the highway. The pickup followed us to South Lake Tahoe, then into Tahoe Keys, a series of islands created by soil dredged from the marsh of the Upper Truckee River. Tennis courts, swimming pools, a pier, a park, miles of channels. Virtually a small city without stores, many of the homes had full-on views of Lake Tahoe.

Margaret opened the door. Her husband, attorney Chuck Stone, fair skinned, came to the slate entryway. We introduced ourselves. Chuck shook Karen's hand, then mine. Margaret invited us in. I handed her a bottle of cabernet recommended by the woman who ran South Lake Tahoe's only high-end wine shop.

In a living room that rivaled that of The Lodge's for square footage, stood Ron Hart and his wife, Eileen. A second round of introductions and handshakes. When asked what we wanted to drink, Karen and I both said we'd take a beer.

Hart said, "Kids these days," and retrieved two bottles as Chuck joined Margaret chopping vegetables in a kitchen that was open to the living room. Copper cooking vessels hung from the ceiling.

Knives chopping onto wood blocks, Margaret said, "We're behind. But we *will* eat."

Karen said, "How can I help?"

"By enjoying yourself."

"Margaret and Chuck rule the kitchen," Eileen said. "Enter at your own risk."

Karen and I sat on a couch that had a worn, fawn-colored cover. Ron and Eileen sat across from us on a twin one. She wore a sleeveless tan dress. Her legs were brown and bare. Ron had on a Hawaiian shirt sporting several shades of brash reds.

He gestured to Karen with his glass. "We understand you're supervising a floor at Barton."

"Half a floor. So far it doesn't look like they'll fire me."

Eileen said, "I bet you're a great addition."

This time Ron moved his drink in a spherical gesture, toward me and back around to his chest. "How's the young doctor?"

"Still waiting for confirmation I passed the boards."

Ron made a sour face. "Don't pretend you're worried. False modesty isn't allowed here. That goes for both of you."

I said, "I'll avoid the kitchen and false modesty."

Margaret shouted over chopping. "Five minutes! Turns out we're not behind." Her silvery hair shined under lights illuminating a six burner gas stove.

Ron said to Karen, "Your husband isn't only an ex basketball star. He cavorts with a super model. Were you with them at the airport, when he was seen in line with Elise Jansen?"

In the kitchen, sizzling sounds. The smell of cooking meat made its way to the living room.

Karen pulled a flank of chestnut hair to in front. "I was visiting family, across the country. Why do you ask?"

"You're not worried Jeff was, you know, hanging around with a famous model?"

"Not at all."

"How is that possible?"

"He's like a Boy Scout. He lives by a code. It doesn't allow adultery."

Eileen threw us a look indicating she knew her husband liked to push people's buttons, get them to react. Margaret invited us to move to the dining room, where Chuck carved a leg of lamb.

Shortly into eating, Chuck said, "Wasn't that horrible, what happened to Jim Stevens?"

I hoped the heat in my cheeks didn't show.

Margaret flashed a palm. "Not tonight. This is a get to know each other meal." She turned to Karen. "Tell us, how did you and Jeff meet?"

"Four years ago, Jeff found my grandfather's wallet. He'd dropped it at the UC Med Center in Sacramento. Inside was a baggy of gold dust, and a piece of paper with my phone number on it. Because sometimes grandpa got lost. Jeff called. He said he could drop off the gold." Karen took a sip of red wine, set the wine glass down. "We met that night."

Eileen said, "You *can't* stop there."

Karen managed to make a long story not too long. It concluded with her and I recovering more than a million dollars in gold dust.

Chuck said, "That was worth the price of admission. Let's have a toast. To love and gold."

Conversation flowed. We had arrived last, we left first, and in the end had a good time.

The pickup followed us. I apologized to Karen for the comments about Elise from future colleague Ron Hart.

Karen said, "In his own way, it was charming."

"I don't think so."

"Certain people can't help themselves from looking foolish sometimes. That's part of their charm."

"I still don't think so."

At the commuter's asphalt parking lot, I cut the engine. Behind us, the pickup truck did the same.

I said, "I get it. He's killed three people. You don't want to come home till he's caught."

Karen said, "How insightful."

Saturday morning my phone rang at nine o'clock sharp. I said hello.

"Jeff, how are you? Steve Spingola, returning your inquiry about the old Cougars. I saw you play for Sac. State. Terrific career."

"We had some good runs."

I remembered Coach Spingola. Enthusiastic, yet controlled. I waited for Spingola to say he was sorry about my hand, and was relieved he didn't mention it. That avoided a distraction.

Spingola said, "Those were great years. I'm retired now."

"Congrats."

Spingola said, "I'm thinking you're interested in getting in touch with one of the guys."

"That's right."

"Which one?"

"I don't remember his name. He was with the team both years we played against you. About six feet, wiry. Number thirty-one."

"Give me a couple minutes."

In less than that, Spingola was back on the phone. "Ken Collins.

Last name begins with C. Same graduating year as you."

"Any contact info?"

"Last time I saw Ken, he came to the gym and wanted to practice with us. He played for me in high school, not just with the Cougars. He went on to play at Bakersfield J.C., then joined the service. He'd filled out quite a bit. I thought it would be good for the team to scrimmage with a guy who'd won a league championship."

"I bet. He was intense."

"It started out great. Ken was in good shape. He pushed the guys. Then he gets beat a couple times, so he gets rough with our best player. It was like Ken had to prove he was better." Spingola hesitated. "No need to go into it. The next day I tell him I checked with the district, and for insurance purposes we couldn't let him practice with us."

"How'd he react?"

"Same as in high school. He stomped off. But that was a long time ago. I hope he's doing well."

I didn't offer speculation as to how or what Collins was doing. "Do you have his parents' address?"

"All I know is, they moved to Seattle. I think they have family there. I don't have any addresses or phone numbers."

"What about the army? Do you know where he was stationed?"

"Fort Benning."

Georgia. Where Brett was confronted by a jerk from the past.

We exchanged a few memories about the old days. I hung up and called the stakeout number. I said I'd be leaving in fifteen minutes for Sacramento to see an old friend, but I was actually driving to Vallejo to try to find Brad Server, fifth place finisher at Cal Ski/Ski, and didn't want South Tahoe PD to know. I'd not received a reply to emails and a phone call I'd made; perhaps Vallejo police had warned Server not to communicate with strangers. I had a street address I thought current. I was going to ask if he'd come across anyone who resembled Mr. Yellow Windbreaker, and generally feel him out, see if he knew anything relevant.

I called Chief Post's private number. As expected, the call went to voice mail. "I have the name of the man who killed Brett and the others. I'm sure of it. Ken Collins. Collins with a C. Age should be thirty-two. I don't have an address but know he grew up in Bakersfield. Dark hair, solid build, a thick scar across his right eyebrow. The guy in the screen shots Stevens distributed statewide."

About to click off, I added, "Chief, I'll never forgive myself for being the reason for today's gathering."

I grabbed a notebook and pen. I had no idea if Server would be home. I was fishing blind, so to speak, but it was all I could think of to do. I locked the door and hustled to the carport. Cold outside, there was a slight breeze. Clouds hovered as if watching for something. With Karen's Volvo gone, the brown Subaru was parked dead center in the carport. Coming around to the driver's side, I pressed the keyless. Door locks squawked. In front of the car, in shadow, rising like a creature from the deep, appeared a man holding a pistol aimed at me.

"You try to run, I'll blow your head off."

In the murky light of the carport, the man's face wasn't clear, but I knew it was Ken Collins. The inevitable confrontation had arrived. I wasn't ready for it. Sweat glistened on the murderer's forehead. All of his clothes were dark.

Collins said, "If you do what I say, you won't get hurt." He shouldered a thick camouflage bag, shaped like a barrel, which looked like what a soldier would carry into battle. "Where you going?"

"To find Brad Server in Vallejo."

"Not anymore." His eyes gleamed like illuminated walnuts.

"They can't see us in here, so don't get any ideas."

Collins, with the gun pointed at me, stepped to the passenger side of the car. "Get behind the wheel. You honk the horn, do anything screwy, you're dead."

Twenty-seven

Collins told me to drop my phone out the driver's window. It clattered on concrete. He climbed in behind the passenger seat, sliding the camouflage pack onto the bench seat. Every time he spoke the pistol rose and fell in snaps as fast as my heart raced. I backed out. Headlights showed a sleeping bag in front of where the Subaru had been parked. Brett's killer knelt low, out of view.

"Keep your eyes straight ahead. Don't even think about looking at the cops' house."

The car curved around tree trunks that lined the road. In what seemed a long while but was less than ten minutes, we reached the highway.

Collins said, "Turn left."

A stakeout officer would check to see if I were followed. Would that person know traveling north on Highway 89 was a significantly longer route to Vallejo? Maybe, but that required a thoroughness that, once it was clear I wasn't being followed, might not be forthcoming.

I drove north through forest. The sounds of tires on asphalt seemed abnormally loud. Collins leaned forward and jammed the gun barrel into my ribs. The lump of scar across and above his right eyebrow was red, raw, like it had been re-cut.

He said, "I didn't recognize you at Sky Lake. But after you put on that country boy act in the bar, you kept showing up in my head. Then it hits me. You were on that team with Boyd. After that, tracking you was easy."

"I didn't recognize you until I watched some old DVDs. They're half our lives ago."

"DVDs? What the hell?"

"Brett's parents made videos of the games. At the end of the season, each player got two DVDs."

"Same old story. A rich kid and his rich parents." Collins blinked against oozing sweat. "I bagged groceries every summer while Boyd went water skiing everywhere with Mommy and Daddy."

"Where we going?" I assumed we'd be going to the gathering for Jim Stevens, but wanted to keep Collins talking, maybe find a way to throw him off track.

Collins said, "Where do you think we're going?"

"Bob La Porte's. He's the closest tournament skier in this direction."

Collins made a dismissive, huffing noise. "La Porte's history. As of whatever time he got to his shop this morning."

I wasn't going to give Collins the warped pleasure of me asking how he'd killed La Porte. I drove slower than the speed limit. Collins didn't seem to notice.

"What made you think I'd be heading out this morning?"

"Of course you're heading out. It's the big Jim Stevens day."

"I really was going to try to find Server, down in Vallejo. Isn't he on your list? Came in fifth. It's like your mission isn't complete."

"Don't tell me about my mission. I've been thinking about something like this for years. It came to me after Cal Ski/Ski. I read about the great Bob La Porte, the great Gary Fingler, the comeback of Brett Boyd. The great Mindy Morris staying even with the guys. I skied all winter in Florida. I got the stats, but people putting the thing on were only interested in names. For sponsorships. The whole thing was about money."

All I could do was keep him talking.

"Why didn't you shoot me at the ski resort? Did you chicken out? I bet you chickened out."

Trees blurred by.

"Was going to shoot you. At the last second I remember that ugly hand of yours. I don't know why, but it made me stop. I decided to keep you living scared. It was good fun. Then this whole thing comes up—it's like a gift—the cop getting killed. It hits me I can put you to use."

"By making me your driver?"

Collins broke into a chortle. "You're going to tell my story. How I've always gotten ripped off by people because they got money or connections."

"Tell me about the belt buckles. For telling your story."

Another chortle. "Guy in the army had one. He couldn't keep his hands off it. You'd think it was his dick. When I was looking for something to use, the belt buckle popped into my head. Pretty cool, huh?"

"You got anymore? Shouldn't you use all of them?"

"I left one as a calling card in the mailbox at La Porte's shop. I'm wearing the last one. Like a going away present to myself."

More trees and granite to the sides. Collins smelled of sweat. He was high on something, and it wasn't brotherly love. I glanced over and saw his eyes pop around like shiny balls in a pinball machine.

"Where'd you get the cyanide?"

Collins scraped a thumbnail over the raw eyebrow scar. "Compliments of a high security location maintained by the United States Army. Been waiting for the right opportunity. Just had to wear PPE and a gas mask, also compliments of the fucking U.S. Army."

Keep him talking.

"How'd it work?"

"Good. You're getting into details. Just before mailing, I'd take a small paintbrush and give the buckle three thick coats of juice. Seal it back in the fancy box right away. Let the post office do their job."

"I was told Morris was through her heater vents."

I looked over. Collins nodded in a kind of reverie. He seemed to be reliving his actions. "Had to be versatile. That one made me the happiest."

Happy was not a word I'd ever pair with Ken Collins.

I said, "If you wanted to put me to use, what was the deal with the fire?"

"Which one?"

"Kamen II. Last week my wife and I almost burned to death running away from it."

I caught a glimpse of Collins ripping at the freshly torn eyebrow scar. "Hey. Slow down. Let me think." I couldn't go much slower. Four cars were stacked up behind us. Collins poked me with the gun barrel. "If you mean that forest fire, you're blaming me for something I had nothing to do with. What the hell would I have against a forest?"

The pistol barrel pressed deeper into my ribs. My heart was getting one hell of a workout.

"Okay," I said. "I believe you."

"Don't put lies out there. This should all be pure truth."

"Pure truth. It's only fair." I looked in the rear-view mirror, hoping to see a police car either following me or heading to the Sky Lake gathering. I could try to get its attention by swerving. "One thing I wonder about," I said, "is why you went to the poisoning scenes and started fires. To destroy evidence?"

Collins broke into a chugging laugh. I caught another glimpse of his eyes. They were filled with merriment. "For the fucking fun of it, man. I liked rubbing it in to the cops. Let them know I was winning."

We passed the dirt road that led to Sky Lake. The gate was open. The two-lane highway curved back and climbed and then curved back again acutely. We reached the ridge. Right and down, Emerald Bay, its water the color of its name.

Collins said, "Go in the campground up on the left."

What if I kept driving? Kept driving up the west shore of Lake Tahoe and ignore his orders to turn around. Would he shoot me? Risk getting snuffed in an accident?

I didn't have the guts to try it.

Collins pulled the gun from my middle. He waved it. "Left here."

I crossed the roadway. We passed two *Campground Closed* signs. They were haphazardly sitting on both sides of the pavement. October, nights too cold for most campers, those who did camp were herded to a campground closer to Emerald Bay. I advanced twenty yards, and halted at a brown iron gate.

The gun poked my ribs again. Its metal found bone. "Turn off the car. Get out slow. Open the gate and come back in. I busted the lock last night."

If I ran, he'd kill me in one shot.

Collins got out and watched me open the gate. I returned to the car.

Once we were both in, he said, "Go to the end. We probably won't have company. If we do, they're history. Simple as that." Again the high-pitched chortle. "See how simple everything is, when you really get down to it?"

The road led us through forest and an empty campground. I stopped at the road's end. My body was in fight or flight mode. The pistol in Collins' hand precluded both of those.

He said, "Get out slow, and easy."

I climbed out of the Subaru. Collins did the same. He kept the pistol aimed at me. He told me to walk ten steps and sit on the dirt, facing away from him, and fold my hands on top of my head. I did this. No one was within sight. I heard Collins slide the camouflage pack onto a shoulder.

"You see the trail," he said. "Let's go. You take off, I'll drop you."

I looked back.

Pistol at eye level, Collins extended his right arm. "I said move it."

The path was wide, flat. I searched for a possible escape route. But if I escaped, Collins would be on his own with whatever was in the pack.

Unlike the slow drive, I walked at a brisk pace. Collins was revved up on something; it might lead to him tripping. If he became fatigued, any move I made would have a better possibility at succeeding. The trail tilted downward. It descended a series of chunky steps formed by rocks. Collins grunted at the effort it took to balance the pack as he let himself down steps that fell more than a foot each. I picked up my pace.

"Slow down, Tater. I already warned you, nothing screwy."

Tater? Not Taylor? He was further out of it than I'd thought.

"Stop. Now."

I stopped. I heard Collins' breaths as he reached me. He struck my right cheek with a fierce blow of the gun barrel. Pain drove me to the ground. Eyes watering, the side of my mouth instantly swelling, I made it to my feet. Sparks quivered in front of me.

Collins said, "I told you to slow down."

The trail flattened, then rose. It became black-pocked granite. No carved-out steps, it was an uphill shelf of smooth rock. If Collins were right behind me, I could spin and, with him balancing the pack, have a chance at sending him down the mountainside.

The path turned steep. I tried to come up with a plan. I drew another anxious blank. Behind me, Collins huffed. The trail ended at granite slabs running back along a plateau. Shortly past them, water ran in narrow shallow stone troughs carved by eons of melted snow. The troughs merged to make Sky Falls, which fell two hundred feet.

Collins shouted, "Stay right there." He puffed hard, coming close behind me. "Take a dozen steps. A little to your left. Butt on the rocks. Keep it there."

I stopped at ten steps, and sat. Overhead, clouds carried strands of darkness, like ribs strung through them. Most of Sky Lake was visible from the perch. At the far end were cabins, the shop and quarters Randy Zim spent summers in, and the sandy volleyball area. Rows of folding chairs faced a wood podium. A black cord ran from the podium to Zim's quarters. What seemed the entire South Lake Tahoe police department was present. About a hundred and fifty people mingled in clumps. Water burbled past me in the granite channels.

Collins seemed half in the moment, half off somewhere in his head. Wheezing, he waved the gun, set it on stone with the barrel pointed at me. He slipped off the pack. He opened its top flap. I looked down at the crowd. Collins pointed to the pistol, in warning. His right arm disappeared inside the pack. In succession Collins extracted a tripod, two sections of an assault rifle, one with a scope, and four ammunition magazines. He turned the bullet packs, one at a time, over in his hand. He examined each one fondly.

I said, "You want me to tell your story. Okay. How long were you in the army?"

"Six years. Six shitty years."

"Any time overseas?"

Collins put the rifle together in workman-like fashion. He swung it up and aimed it at me—I hopped backwards. Collins cackled. He snapped his head, flicking sweat.

"You see any combat?"

Collins shook his head. "Naw." He loaded a magazine. It made a popping sound. "I was an instructor at Fort Benning. Master Sergeant. Marksmanship."

"Why was it lousy?"

Collins looked from his equipment to me and back as he continued to set up.

"I didn't kiss ass, so they wouldn't give me my due. I should've been running the program."

Collins' eyes squeezed together, opened. He reached into a front pocket of his jeans. Out came a small purple vial with a white cap but no prescription label. Collins opened it, tipped it into his mouth, tossed the plastic vial aside.

He said, "Don't you dare move."

Collins stepped ahead, scooped running water and swallowed whatever was in his mouth.

"What's that you're taking? For your story."

"I haven't slept worth shit in a month. Understand? Don't mislead people. I'm not a user. This is an exception."

A small bird, black-headed with yellow-green tail feathers, whizzed by at eye level and out beyond the waterfall. Collins lurched to the pistol. He spun around but of course there was no threat. He set the pistol on dry stone. Its barrel pointed toward me.

"Tomorrow I'll be more famous than Boyd, Fingler, Morris, La Porte, more famous than all of 'em put together in a big black hole. I got my stats for this year, water and snow, written down. You'll find 'em later."

"You don't really want to do this. It's just a fantasy. You've had it so long you think it's real. It's not. Stop."

"Shut your mouth. Can you see the whole show down there?"

I saw more than a hundred souls gathered together to honor a public servant. Their lives were about to be shattered. "Don't do it, Ken. Why go after all these people you've never even met?"

Collins smirked. "Why not? I finally get something big, no matter how many times they cheated me out of my due."

"Who cheated you?"

"Shut up and listen. I do this and go down the falls. People will catch it on video because they'll hear shots first. They got TV people down there. It'll be epic."

His whole face relaxed. A beatific smile brought light to his cheeks. Collins picked up the tripod. Looking back every few seconds, he stepped toward the top of the waterfall, found a spot to wedge in the tripod legs. His shoes were in shallow, gurgling water. Collins tested the tripod's steadiness. He inserted the rifle into its slot.

Collins turned around, stepped, retrieved the pistol and stuck it in the right front pocket of jeans.

"You can see good, right?"

"Yeah. Fine. But tell me more of your story. I want to give you your due."

From below, echoing up the mountainside: "Testing. Testing. One more testing." Chief Post stood at the lectern. He rose his arms in a kind of benediction. "Friends, please be seated. Thank you to everyone for coming today."

The words echoed up the mountain.

A jubilant Collins: "Show time!"

Below and ahead, tiny-looking people took seats in orderly rows. Many remained standing as there weren't enough chairs. Their backs were to Collins and me. Beyond them was forest, and beyond that the dreamy cobalt-blue of Lake Tahoe.

Collins went to the ammunition magazines. He slid one in his left front pocket, one in each of his back pockets. He spoke serenely. "Tell 'em how disciplined I was. Tell 'em how disciplined I was right to the end."

Below, Chief Post thanked a few people by name. I ceased listening. Every part of me concentrated on the man who murdered Brett. He hunched. He assessed the balance of the rifle on the tripod. He leaned forward. Collins dried his right hand on the front of a dark long-sleeved shirt.

I don't remember leaving the granite.

Collins tipped the rifle up—and I drove my head into the center of his back. Bullets exploded. My hands slammed into him and drove Collins ahead, pumping my legs as hard as I could. He lost his footing. Gunfire roared. I drove my feet into water-covered granite and forced Collins forward with every ounce of my being. I wanted him dead.

From below came terrified shrieks. I screamed and thrust my body forward and fell as Collins went over the falls, dragging the rifle and tripod. He skidded face first down steep wet granite. No more bullets fired.

The wailing below persisted.

My upper body past the precipice, hands in running water, I closed my eyes and clasped wet stone. My left foot plunked into one of the stone channels. I slithered my right foot in vain, not locating another slot to gain purchase.

To move back and up, I pushed my hands against granite—and slid forward a couple of inches. To stop myself from going over I wedged my left foot in the stone trough at a more extreme angle. I felt for a better hold with my half hand, using thumb and forefinger to keep me in place.

I opened my eyes. At the far end of the lake people fled. Half of them raced toward cabins, half raced into forest. Their aggregate panic and fear reached me. I *felt* it. I closed my eyes, to concentrate. My shoes filled with water. Cold water began filling my sweatshirt at the belly. Water inflated my left pants leg like a balloon.

I gave pushing upwards another try. My weight and the downward tilt of my body were too much to overcome. I spit out cold water.

Twenty minutes. That was my guess as to how long it would take officers to drive to the end of the campground road and run to where the shots came from. That was the only route from Sky Lake to the top of Sky Falls.

Maybe twenty-five minutes.

Pain that started in my contorted left ankle traveled up my leg. I told myself to focus on hands and feet holding steady. My mind wouldn't obey.

I remembered being trapped in the fire, orange light closing over me and Karen like the lid of a coffin. I remembered the snow-melt water heating up as flames passed overhead. I remembered wandering, alone as a boy, among redwood trees that are some of the oldest living things on earth. I remembered crouching behind a log, listening to the hiss of the sea. The mist covering me tasted of salt.

I thought of Karen's grandfather, saintly Clyde Whitney. He believed in the perfection of the universe.

I whispered, "Karen."

Whispering her name brought me back to the present. I clung to wet granite. Water ran into my clothes, subtly lifting me.

Eyes closed, I saw Karen's face. I'd try to see Karen's face until I dropped into blackness.

Running water lifted my right leg above the granite. Held in place by my hands and left foot, I was visited by a kind of white noise that numbed me. Next, my mind's eye saw only white. No shapes, no movement. I thought it an involuntary prelude indicating my time was up. The last light before the plunge.

Head drooping forward, I sensed the fall. It was a quiet fall. Nothing hurt. Nothing scraped. I tried to remember something but couldn't think of what it was. Over and over, I tried to retrieve what I couldn't remember.

I switched to checking in with hands and feet, pressing them onto what I knew was stone under the blank screen of whiteness. It was as if my hands and feet were wet sponges. How much longer before running water pushed me over?

I didn't faint, but floated in a dazed stupor.

A male voice broke the trance. "South Tahoe PD. Don't move. Don't move at all."

It was like waking up in another part of the country and not knowing where you are. Still mostly in white emptiness, I said, "I made it over okay?"

"Seriously, man. Don't move. We'll each take an ankle. When I say 'now,' raise your chin without moving anything else."

A different male voice: "Don't fight it. You fight it, we'll lose you."

Four hands took hold of my two ankles. Someone said "now," and I was yanked backwards over granite, chin bouncing, my middle strained, my life saved.

A minute later, the three of us were sprawled back where the stone rivulets were several feet apart before merging into Sky Falls. The view brought me back to where we were. And what had happened. Officers Jones and Araujo were as sapped as I was. In halting gulps, I reported the last minute of Ken Collins' life.

Officer Jones spoke into a tiny speaker clamped to the pocket of his uniform shirt. He told Chief Post I'd pushed Collins over the falls just as he pulled the trigger on an automatic rifle.

Chief Post's voice crackled in poor, high-country reception. "It's about damn time he did something good."

I said to Jones, "Can I talk to him?"

Jones spoke into the tiny speaker. "Can he?"

"He's earned it. People are scared as hell, but calming down. No known rounds reached here."

Officer Ron Jones sat next to me. He unhooked a wire from his pocket, stretched the little speaker toward me. I told Post that Collins had killed the skiers in a long-fantasized series of revenge acts. I recounted his plan for a slaughter designed to make him infamous.

I said, "Collins didn't start Kamen II. I'm pretty sure it was a guy named William Whitmer."

I described seeing Whitmer with binoculars up on that ridge, looking down at Sky Lake as Brett's chalet smoldered. I told Post that Whitmer was Brett's drug dealer. With the Kamen II fire, I'd been snooping around and Whitmer may have decided to get rid of me.

"I'll explain it better later."

Next I told Post I believed Roberto Ramirez was a major source of fentanyl and methamphetamine in the region. "I have pictures, dates and times. Again, more later."

A few seconds passed. Water gurgled in the granite troughs. My head seemed stuffed with cotton.

Post said, "Jeff?"

"Yeah?"

"From now on, you stay the hell out of my business."

"No problem."

Twenty-eight

Because of Karen's medical training, and perhaps because media people swarmed Barton Memorial Hospital, the doctors released me late that afternoon. I made a statement to the police detailing everything that happened with Collins, and what I knew about Whitmer and Roberto. I agreed to a request from Chief Post, delivered as an order, not to talk to anyone about the events that transpired after I'd read about Brett's death. I was told to not eat solid food because I had a cracked chin bone and because in response to the pistol blow my right jaw looked like a boiled lobster. My ankle was badly sprained; an X-ray showed no broken bones.

Rather than leave my car in the woods, Officer Nick Araujo had driven it to the back parking lot at the police station. I hadn't noticed Collins placing an envelope on the back seat. Araujo saw it.

Early that evening, in a press conference I watched online, Chief Post described an envelope that contained a list of Collins' grievances, from being taken out of basketball games in high school when his team became far ahead and, according to Collins, thereby robbing him of more points and scholarship offers. Five dates of his time in the army were listed as Collins being unfairly passed over for promotions. Three dates were listed where, post military, he claimed he'd been unfairly fired from private security firms. The run-ins with Brett were described as Brett preventing him from entering water ski tournaments because Brett feared Collins would beat him. His parents were not spared. They were cited as telling Collins he "Didn't have it," like older brother Jason did. Collins did not elaborate on what he thought that meant.

Chief Post said no written statement accompanied the list. The only material other than the list of grievances were sheets of paper documenting snow and water ski slalom scores Collins made in amateur tournaments during the previous year. Written on them was *Proof they cheated me out of Cal Ski/Ski.*

Saturday I was a hero. Collins' four ammunition magazines contained thirty rounds each. It would have been a bloodbath.

My phone didn't break when dropped in the carport, but I answered few calls or texts. They came nonstop; I turned off the phone's sound. I answered Elise's voice message—she'd seen what happened on the news—by texting thanks but I wasn't communicating with people. Voice mail requests for an interview came from the major networks; more cable networks than I knew existed; newspapers far and wide; gun safety groups; and more. I deleted them. I thought about how prominent politicians and celebrities live in that kind of whirlwind, how some get hooked on the attention and can't feel fulfilled without it.

The police blocked off Cathedral Road. Two officers patrolled the area around the cabin, sending back interlopers of one type or another.

Karen's phone rang so often she shut if off altogether.

Clint Sherman called. I saw his name and answered. I asked if he'd ever killed anyone.

"I've been lucky that way. Let's talk about you."

Clint let me babble about feeling like my head was stuffed with cotton. I asked if he had any advice.

"Situations like this can mess with your head. Pay attention to that kind of stuff. I'm here for you. Whatever you need."

La Porte's hand was seriously burned, but he was otherwise not injured when a homemade pipe bomb fizzled as he opened the aluminum garage door of his workshop in Tahoe City.

My mom called from Crescent City, on the coast near the Oregon border. She was visiting a childhood friend who worked at the prison there. I asked if media people were hounding her.

"They don't have the number yet. They got the landline, at home. Del's telling them you flew to Argentina on a private jet. He says nobody knows where you are except President Biden. He's having a ball with this."

"Mom, when they catch up to you, don't answer any questions. Don't let them coax you into talking about me. Anything you say will get twisted."

"You're a hero. You saved dozens of lives. A hundred."

"You don't know everything. I'm not a hero."

"Yes you are. Families will thank you forever."

Mom said goodbye. I looked at my phone. I knew then that the unusual circumstances of my upbringing, followed by all those years apart with scant communication, meant I'd never be close to the only immediate family I had. This didn't sadden me. What I experienced was detachment from everything. My body felt hollow.

In Sunday's *Tahoe Daily Tribune*, an article cited Elise's telling Chief Post what happened with Gummer at her house, including me striking a helpless man and the embarrassment to Gummer of urinating in his pants. The article ended with Gummer's threat to get revenge on me that I'd relayed to Post, and a recounting of Stevens' head on collision with him.

On Monday, Post held a second press conference. He announced that an anonymous tip had come in, tying local electrician William Whitmer to igniting the Kamen II fire. In the course of their investigation, South Tahoe PD found materials consistent with arson activity. In the attic at Whitmer's house, police located hidden caches of drugs at a volume suggesting he was a dealer. He had been arrested, Post said, and made bail with the help of a bondsman.

There was no mention of Roberto. I figured South Tahoe PD had called in the Feds. Drugs had crossed state lines. The Feds would be seeking to trace where Roberto's supply originated from.

Every question to Post about Ken Collins, and me, was deflected. Post said he'd provide more information later at an un-named date.

I was told to document any death threats. There were three, along with a dozen voice messages informing me I wasn't welcome in South Lake Tahoe, and if I were smart I'd get out of town.

I didn't hear from Margaret Field. So I called and said we needed to talk. She asked where I'd like to meet.

"Let's do it over the phone. I'd be trailed by reporters. You don't want them following you after, asking questions."

Margaret said, "I'm okay with the phone."

"My hunch is you can guess where this is heading."

"I've never been good at predicting the future."

Not cold, yet less than lukewarm.

"I can't practice in the Tahoe area. Sure, the threats and harassment would eventually pass, but I can't imagine ever feeling welcome. Maybe I shouldn't be. Jim Stevens was a local hero, and I'm the reason he's gone."

"You just made things simpler for me. Your actions with the man who crashed into Jim, they're inexcusable. Slapping him around in that model's house?" Her voice rose in pitch. "I didn't really know Jim Stevens. But if we had a patient where there were suspicions of abuse at home, he was the go-to guy. He was discreet."

"I know what I did hurt a lot of people."

"You acted heroically. Who knows how many lives you saved. At the same time, we can't bring you on board."

Her decision finalized, Margaret moved on to the personal. She asked how Karen was holding up.

"She's hanging in there. She insists on going to work every day."

"Because she's a winner."

We said goodbyes. I went outside, hobbled across the back deck and looked down at the dark lake. It was unusually cold for mid October. I stood, dormant, paralyzed of mind. The season's first snow fell for some time before I noted it on the deck railing. I went inside and watched snow fall.

Karen came home. She hugged me. She found enough to eat. I swallowed a liquid meal. Karen's cheeks drooped, as did her usual flagpole posture. Karen said goodnight before eight o'clock.

My laptop screen appeared murky. I re-read praise for stopping a slaughter. I grew disgusted with myself. Was I another electronic addict? Yes. I logged off. I stood at the back windows, the outdoor light on, watching the snow pile up.

Karen came into the room. "Are you okay?"

"I don't know."

I'd lost track of the days. I just knew it was some days after killing another human being, and that had come shortly after indirectly causing two others to die in a head-on collision. Everything looked askew. The floor seemed tilted. I looked at the piece of cardboard taped over the shot-through window. My thoughts didn't connect.

"Let's keep each other warm," Karen said. She led me to the hall and toward our bedroom.

I stopped. "I'm sorry for everything. And the money, for the lease."

"Forget it. We'll go back and start over."

Karen meant return to Sacramento. She'd easily find a job. She had informed her supervisors at Barton Memorial of her plans. I'd see where I could land.

I said, "You sure you're okay with this?"

"If I weren't," Karen said, "you'd know."

"That's true."

Karen kissed the palm of her hand. She touched it to my forehead, avoiding the still-swollen cheek. She nudged me into walking again, and led me to the bedroom.

"Try to get some sleep. We'll start packing in the morning."

I didn't sleep. As soon as I heard Karen's faint snore, I returned to The Lodge's great room. The fire had petered out. I looked at the blank laptop screen.

I pictured the crowd who'd come to Sky Lake to pay their respects to Jim Stevens. They came because of how he'd conducted his life.

I went down the hallway to our bedroom. I asked Karen to come with me. I wandered back to the great room and stared outside at snow and tree trunks with slits of blackness between them.

Karen put an arm around my waist. "I'm worried about you."

"Let's not go. It'll take years, but we can make a life here. We can help people."

"Jeff, your emotions are all over the place."

"You have a good job. You know they'll keep you on. I'll try with local clinics. I'll do yard work if I have to. Anything but run away."

Karen said, "There's so much to deal with." Her eyes searched mine. She seemed to be checking on my stability, perhaps my reliability. "How would you do it?"

"By re-lighting the fire. Replacing that window. By refusing to feel sorry for myself, like with my hand. Other than that, I don't know."

About the Author

Scott Lipanovich lives in Santa Rosa, California. Stories of his have appeared in *Ireland's Fish Story Prize, The Seattle Review, Crosscurrents, Defiant Scribe, Abiko* (Japan), *Wild Duck Review, Ridge Review, Gold and Treasure Hunter Magazine, Summerfield Journal,* and several anthologies. In film, he has worked with two Academy Award winners, and two multiple Emmy-winning producers.

Scott is the author of the Jeff Taylor Mysteries, *The Lost Coast* (July 2021), *The Golden Ceiling* (July 2022), and *Sky Lake* (July 2023). He's working on the next novel in the series.

If you enjoyed this book,
please consider writing a review
and sharing it with other readers.

Many of our authors are happy to participate in
Book Club and Reader Group discussions.
For more information, contact us at info@encirclepub.com.

Thank you,
Encircle Publications

For news about more exciting new fiction, join us at:

Facebook: www.facebook.com/encirclepub

Instagram: www.instagram.com/encirclepublications

Sign up for the Encircle Publications newsletter:
eepurl.com/cs8taP